TOTAL CONSTANT ORDER

CRISSA-JEAN CHAPPELL

HARPER TEEN
Katherine Tegen Books
An Imprint of HarperCollins*Publishers*

HarperTeen is an imprint of HarperCollins Publishers.

Total Constant Order
Copyright © 2007 by Crissa-Jean Chappell

Library of Congress Cataloging-in-Publication Data
Chappell, Crissa-Jean.
Total constant order / Crissa-Jean Chappell.— 1st ed.
p. cm.
"HarperTeen."
Summary: Resentful and upset when her family moves from Vermont to Miami,
Florida, and her parents' fighting escalates, high-schooler Fin develops obsessive-
compulsive disorder (OCD), becoming consumed with numbers and counting,
irrational worrying, and avoiding germs.
ISBN 978-0-06-088605-9 (trade bdg.) — ISBN 978-0-06-088606-6 (lib. bdg.)
[1. Obsessive-compulsive disorder—Fiction. 2. Emotional problems—Fiction. 3.
Miami (Fla.)—Fiction.] I. Title.
PZ7.C37275To 2007   2006102964
[Fic]—dc22   CIP
                                                                       AC

2 3 4 5 6 7 8 9 10

First Edition

For Mom and Dad

Contents

Part 1: September

Part 2: October

Part 3: November

Part 4: December

S E P T E M B E R

19 5 16 20 5 13 2 5 18

Volcanoes

In ninth grade, I learned that the world is made of lava. My science teacher, Ms. Armstrong, illustrated this fact with candy corn.

"One, two, three," she counted, crunching each color. "Crust, mantle, core."

I munched the stale, waxy-tasting candy and gawked at the pictures in my earth science textbook. I thought about volcanoes belching, stars exploding. It's a wonder people didn't stumble around, knocking into one another.

I slouched in the front row, drawing stars on my desk. My nearsighted eyes had grown so bad, I was legally blind without contacts. The blackboard shimmered. I squeezed my pencil into my palm, leaving pointy marks that hurt and felt nice at the same time. I clamped my hands extra hard when Ms. Armstrong called my name.

"Fin, are you paying attention?" she asked.

She didn't know the truth: I paid attention to everything.

On the outside, I was quiet and still. Inside, I was churning. Nobody could guess what was happening inside my head. I was trying to control the beat of my wiggling desk, the spaces in the whispers around me, the rhythm of Ms. Armstrong's creaky footsteps. Numbers, with their constant order, would do the trick.

I counted backward: five, four, three, two, one. Every star I drew had an odd number of points, though for some reason this didn't bug me. It was like making a wish. When I finished, I leaned back in my chair, putting a punctuation mark at the end of my ritual.

The desk wobbled figure eights whenever I shifted my weight. You could tell it had been a living thing at one point. I tried guessing its age by counting rings, the tree's fingerprints. Too many students had scratched their current love interests into its planetary whirls. I thought about all those names drilled throughout time. Together, they added up to nothing.

With my pen, I traced my thumb on the desk. After the right hand (which always came first), I would trace the left, making sure my fingers added up to ten. I could feel the thick stare of Ms. Armstrong, aimed in my direction.

"Young lady," Ms. Armstrong said. "All six feet on the floor."

This meant the chair's feet as well as my own. I thought of a rumor I'd heard about a boy who had leaned his chair back too far and fell. He had split his noggin, watermelon style, after plunging to the rock-hard floor of the classroom next door.

That's when she noticed my drawings.

"Who did this?" she asked.

I shrugged.

"Did you deface school property?"

I thought about that word, "de-face." The desk didn't have a face until I gave it one.

"What is this about?" Her eyes swept across my felt-tipped cosmos.

I didn't have a clue.

"Why?" she wanted to know.

Who? What? Why? I strung their letters together like a chain: three, four, three.

I had no answers. But I was smart enough to know that something was wrong with me. Until I figured out what it was, I'd keep quiet.

Ms. Armstrong clucked her tongue. She gave me a note to take home. I folded it five times and stuffed it in my book bag.

During lunch, I was left alone in the classroom. Ms. Armstrong made me wipe down all the desks with Windex—an activity that I converted into a new ritual. I would spray twice, wipe three times, and count again.

In the back were three floor-to-ceiling bulletin boards. Ms. Armstrong had covered them in a giant *National Geographic* map of the Everglades. Our desks were shaped in a double **U** to invite class discussion. We had only one skinny window. It was smothered with cactus plants, as if looking there were dangerous.

Outside the boys were playing tennis. Every so often, the ball whacked against the window, which Ms. Armstrong had covered with two strips of duct tape. A giant **X**. My teacher was a worrier too. She always wore a hat to shield off cancerous solar rays. The class made bets on when she'd take it off. She never took it off.

Whack, whack. One, two. I got up and peeked out the window. For some reason, their idea of tennis involved a lot of running around the court. To them, it was baseball with rackets.

I flicked the light switch a couple times. Something made me go around the room and touch all the corners. It was like being trapped in a box. The only way I could climb out was through counting. I eased myself into Ms. Armstrong's chair, swiveling back and forth . . . one, two . . . one, two . . . making windshield-wiper noises. I was listening hard to the noise in my head.

On her desk I found a photo of her middle-age son puffing on a trombone. Ms. Armstrong said he'd performed for the Queen of England. This didn't mean much to our country. Forever he'd blow a note that nobody could hear. Forever was a long time. Infinity. The only number whose size and shape I couldn't imagine.

In back of the picture frame were two bolts. I touched them once, twice, then unscrewed them. The photo fluttered out. I noticed that one of the corners was torn, as if a giant roach had taken a bite out of it. I considered ripping the other corner, just to make it even. The thought grabbed hold and wouldn't let go. I felt that familiar pressure building inside me. Before I realized it, my fingers were busy shredding. But the bottom half needed to match, so I tore it, too. When I tried to stuff it back inside the frame, it no longer fit, so I tore the entire thing to bits.

I tucked the empty frame in Ms. Armstrong's drawer. I opened my desk and dumped the shreds inside. As I slammed it shut, I noticed faint outlines of my stars and comets in number two pencil. Even after wiping the desk down, I couldn't see myself in its shine, as the TV ads promised. Smudges clouded the surface. Rust bubbled down the desk's legs like barnacles. You could cut yourself on them.

The tennis-ball noise didn't go away. It grew so loud, I looked out the window. And then I saw him. The weird boy, Thayer Pinsky, who carried an inhaler everywhere and never stopped coughing. Nobody sat next to him on the picnic bench. Not that he seemed to care. He wore jeans so baggy their cuffs dragged on the floor. His dreadlocked hair was the color of sun-bleached grass. In his hand he clenched a fat Magic Marker. He was hunched over the bench, scribbling away.

Like the rest of the freshmen in Miami Dade High, I avoided Thayer. I'd heard that he wasn't a real student. He was a much older actor rehearsing the role for a cable movie. That would explain why he always brought a tape recorder to class. I was thinking so hard, trying to organize my brain, that I forgot to keep counting. The other players were flinging the ball, letting it bounce off the wall behind him.

Sharon Lubbitz came and joined the boys. She could shoot a ball far. She had roofed a few that the janitor had to fetch down. Now she was beaming it at Thayer, the human target. He didn't even look up.

I leaned against the window, with its masking-tape **X**. The urge to peel off the tape burned inside my fingers. Before I could begin, I saw the weird kid snatch the ball out of the air. He didn't toss it back to them, no matter how much they yelled.

Maybe he was the boy who had tilted too far in his chair.

The others waited on the court. Then Thayer pitched the ball sideways. The window above Ms. Armstrong's desk exploded into jagged pieces. Glass spilled out of the frame, along with curly strips of masking tape. The ball was lost somewhere inside the classroom. I couldn't help looking for it, despite the shards twinkling across the floor like cool, clear water.

I watched Sharon and the boys run, scattering into corners. Thayer got up and walked away.

It was 12:53 in the afternoon. Lunch was over, detention done. A hundred and seventy-seven minutes to go.

Swimming

I was drawing in the bathroom, counting stars on the wall and waiting for P.E. to end. Sketching was the best way I could control the noise in my head. For me, all numbers had rhythm. For example, I could have traveled to the moon on the number eight, which soared with the speed of a rocket. Zero drifted in space.

Three was the pace of planet Earth, spinning on its axis. We lived three planets away from the sun, in three dimensions. Everywhere I looked, I saw threes. I kept count like a magic spell. I counted my footsteps, my breath, and even my heart thudding under my ribs. If I didn't keep count, I worried that it would stop beating.

In late September, we were finally beginning our

swimming course. The school's pool was Gatorade green, despite the gallons of chlorine they dumped in it. After dog paddling for an hour, my eyes reddened and burned. For the rest of the day, my hair would stink. I could almost picture the fumes, like quivery lines in cartoons.

After P.E., I quickly changed in the nearest bathroom stall. I stared at the unflushed toilet filled with someone else's pee. Smelling it made me feel like contaminated molecules were infiltrating my body. I scooted into another stall.

The bathroom door slammed.

A herd of jock girls poured in. I'd recognize their Nike-clad footsteps anywhere. It was Sharon and her clones—Jessica Conway and Colleen Hurst. They wore sneakers studded with metal spikes. Their hair was braided like rope. But these jocks turned heads, even with a mouthful of metal.

I came out and washed my hands. I wanted to sniff them, just to make sure they were clean, but Sharon, the alpha female, was waiting. My fingers still felt germy. I needed to wash them again.

She pushed me. "Get out of my face."

I wanted to say something, but my mouth wouldn't work. I pumped some liquid soap. One, two, three. Scrubbed for three seconds. Rinsed until my skin tingled.

"Move, you stupid freak."

She tapped my arm, making me lose count. This meant that I had to start over. One, two, three.

Sharon reached for the soap. The lid clattered on the floor and sloshed pink ooze. Now what?

"I said *move*." Sharon shoved me aside. She turned the faucet on full blast.

I wanted to yank her braid and twist it around her throat and tell her to stop acting like a mutant. She didn't know what it was like, having to perform these stupid rituals. My hands tingled.

"Hey, Fin," said Sharon. "If you didn't wear those ghetto hoop earrings, you wouldn't look like a chonga from Hialeah."

If anyone looked like a "chonga," a girl who rolled with the thugs at Dolphin Mall, it was Sharon, who cinched the waistband of her miniskirts to make them even shorter. One minute, hoop earrings dangled from every girl's earlobes in first period.

Now they belonged in the same category as bangle bracelets or claw-length fingernails. I couldn't keep up with the rules. They always changed.

Sharon kept talking. "No guy is ever going to ask you out."

Before we moved here last year, when my family lived in Vermont, I had what Mama called male buddies. I had played with all the boys in kindergarten, my brief moment of popularity. They invited me to come over and battle Sega games like the Mean Bean-Steaming Machine and Sonic the Hedgehog. The only game the girls wanted to play was House. It seemed like a big waste of time. I'd join them only if they'd let me be the family dog. Out of all the things you could imagine, I couldn't believe they'd pretend to be grown-ups.

Back in the ladies' room, Sharon was telling me to pluck my eyebrows.

"Yeah, her eyebrows are major," said Jessica.

They talked about me in the third person, like I wasn't even there.

"Do you think she cuts her own hair?" said

Sharon. "Or does her mommy cut it for her?"

"She's probably had the same hairstyle since first grade," Jessica added.

It was true. My dirty blond hair was geometric, as if a scissors-wielding maniac had plopped a salad bowl on my head and snipped around it. I was wearing my stupid black denim skirt and a Members Only jacket. At my old school, nobody would've cared. Here, girls got suspended for wearing low-rider jeans and showing off their belly buttons.

"Her skin is so pale. You can, like, see the veins in her wrists and everything," Sharon said.

I stared at the pink ooze on the floor. I wanted to scream all the craziness out of me. Instead, I counted to three and pushed past the girls. As I slammed the door, I could still hear them laughing.

Technicolor Apocalypse

My mother didn't teach me to count. She didn't zip flash cards in front of my nose. I taught myself what I needed to know: Thirty days has September, a spoonful of sugar makes the medicine go down.

Mama taught me to draw. She bought number two pencils and Mr. Sketch Markers that smelled of licorice. I practiced on paper bags: *F* for Frances. *I* for Isabelle. *N* for Nash.

I was named after Mama. Fin is her nickname for me. It means the end.

"The end of what?" I'd ask.

"Of children," she'd say. "I told your father, I'm not having a baby. I'm having a hamster." This was her idea of a joke.

By the time I was born, my parents had traded their high school rings for wedding bands. Dad wanted to christen me Noël since I was born on Christmas Eve. Mama toted me home from the hospital in a fur-lined stocking. That night it snowed. When we lived in Vermont, it used to snow all the time. That was before Dad dragged us to Miami and everything changed.

Mama said I was a surprise. I knew exactly what she meant. I had her washed-out blue eyes but I didn't see things like she did. I had her mouth, which required brute force to keep shut, but we spoke a different language.

Mama said, "At least you got your father's giraffe eyelashes."

Did giraffes have eyelashes?

Dad used to joke, "Would you rather have a million dollars or Fin's head full of pennies?"

I couldn't even count that high.

Mama said he was full of it. She called me her magnum opus.

"Promise this," she whispered. "Don't grow."

I must have grown. Even Mama's high school

yearbook photo looked nothing like me now. Signatures circled the margins of the book like closed captions.

David is the class clip. In physics, he's a pip.

I studied the photo of David, a sweaty boy with a military crew cut. He might've been thinking, "Try to make me show my teeth."

"Who's that, Mama? Your boyfriend?"

"Your father," she said.

During the warm, yellow summers, Dad took me for walks along Lake Champlain. I would dawdle along, my bare feet slapping the shore, a moon terrain of misplaced junk.

"Look," I told him. "Look, look." Dad would look at whatever I excavated from the dirt—rusty soda tabs, a necklace of fishing lures with realistic eyes.

One afternoon, I stepped on a hornet's nest. Dad slapped mud on the swelling.

"That's what Indians do," he told me.

I hiccupped and sobbed and finally believed him.

Dad carried me home on his shoulders. When

we ducked through the door, Mama said the hornet was his fault. After that, we didn't go for walks anymore.

Before we moved to Miami, I'd always heard a voice in my head ordering me to listen. The rules changed constantly. Once, I spent an entire day stepping over cracks. Another time, the voice told me to enter every room with my right foot forward. If I forgot and used my unlucky left, I started over. When I heard my parents arguing, I tapped the light switch on and off to keep us safe.

I was always in danger of doing something wrong.

My Instinctive Reality

I slept with my dad's old-school Walkman under my pillow, just to muffle the static between my ears. I tucked the blanket around me, all four corners. But nothing seemed to help.

My chest felt clogged. I checked my alarm clock. According to its glow-in-the-dark digits, I had slept two hours and sixteen minutes. I grabbed my bathrobe, shrugged into the sleeves, and padded across the tile floor.

There were fourteen steps from my bedroom to the office. Fourteen was an even number, so I was okay. I sat in front of Dad's old computer. The keyboard sounded extra clackity as I typed in my password: Damnitall. My only e-mails were spam:

"Receive good luck within thirty days.

If you do not forward this letter to

ten friends, you will suffer a horrible misfortune."

If I had already "received good luck," how could things go wrong? Since I didn't have ten friends, I hit delete.

My eyes burned from lack of sleep. I considered going back to bed. I could try cough medicine, but I refused to take it, in case I nodded off and never woke up. I knew it sounded crazy, but I couldn't stop worrying. I turned on the TV, hoping it would take my mind off the squeezing in my chest.

The Weather Channel. Mama's favorite. A frizzy anchorwoman stood in the rain, screaming into her mike. "It's really blowing out here." I hated the way newscasters talked about storms. They sounded like Ms. Armstrong gushing over the "elegance" of natural selection.

Me, I preferred the elegance of counting. Not that my number obsession helped in the algebra department, where letters symbolized entire equations. It didn't do much for earth science either, where I had already failed a test with a big fat zero. The note from Ms. Armstrong was crumpled at the bottom of my book bag. I had to hide it from Mama.

I turned off the TV and I hopped on my bike, even though it was dark and the sky had started to sprinkle. I pedaled around the neighborhood, counting alligator walls. Those are what people built to keep reptiles out of their backyards. There were six.

The sidewalk was dusty and cracked. I could feel pearls of sweat sliding down my neck. I cruised past burned-looking lawns and a cartoonish row of mailboxes. One was a headless parrot that looked as though it might flap its feathered wings and take off, giving new meaning to the term "air mail." Next came a squat, concrete manatee, clutching the mailbox in its mitteny flippers.

In Vermont, I could bike for miles without seeing another house. In Miami, it's all cinder block malls, sweltering parking lots, intersecting freeways, roads, and lanes that Mama calls "urban sprawl."

There's no decent bus or rail system, and the Metrorail, an aboveground subway, shuttles back and forth on a single line. Our suburb, Kendall, is filled with flat, manicured lawns and pools sparkling in the backyards. You won't find many parks. Except those that charge admission.

My parents had fought for as long as I could remember, but they didn't split up until a couple months ago, a year after we moved here. I could've blamed the move for all their drama, but I knew better. If I had seen this move coming, I would've locked myself in the bathroom, the way freaky people barricaded themselves after reading a horoscope marinated in doom and gloom: "Lie low, play waiting game."

I biked around identical, quasi-Mediterranean houses, the windows **X**'ed with masking tape, as if that would protect them from hurricanes. You could buy shutters shaped like metal accordions. They were mucho expensive. Our house, with its maze of sliding glass doors, was too complicated for that kind of store-bought, Home Depot convenience. We stuck to old-fashioned plywood. Some people kept them up year-round. I couldn't believe that they were willing to live in the dark, always worrying about the next storm.

By the time I got home, it was pouring. Mama was bustling around the kitchen, checking everything a million times—the stove, the lights, the ever-present leaks. Maybe insomnia was passed down in my genes.

"Is there a reason you're riding your bike at two in the morning?" she asked.

I stood, dripping all over the floor. "I needed some air."

Mama glared. "Couldn't you get some air in here?"

The house smelled like leftovers—the highlight of the refrigerator—something fried and reheated. Dad was better at domestic details. He used to cook all our meals. He taught me the definition of al dente pasta: If it sticks to the wall, it's done. Once Mama took over, my school lunches were green apples shoved in grocery bags. She gave me a couple dollars to buy a peanut butter and jelly sandwich from the cafeteria. Dinner was "smush"—a dish that consisted of canned peas on instant rice—until I taught myself to cook from the back pages of *Better Homes* (meaning better homes than yours). Mama still ate tuna from the can, like a cat.

And her control-freakishness was getting on my nerves. She never sat still. Mama dragged every portable container we owned and dumped them like a tag sale in the living room. I stared at a fondue pot about to overflow with rainwater.

"Candles?" Mama asked, looking around. "In case the lights go out."

I told her to check the pantry.

"Pantry?" Mama repeated, as if she'd never heard the word before.

Did we have a pantry? The word sounded odd— almost dirty, four-lettered.

Mama leaned across the table and fired up a cigarette. Despite the heat, she wore sweatpants that hung off the skinny handles of her hips. That's one thing we have in common: our head-bumping height and lack of curves. Mama is a sharp, bony woman.

Goop shone in her hair, which was scraped into a ponytail. I wanted to wear my hair long, but Mama said it tangled too easily.

Mama took a drag and coughed so hard, I could

hear froth in her throat.

"Fin, we need to have a discussion," she said.

I counted the freckles below her collarbone. God, why couldn't I have freckles? "Right now?" I asked.

She nodded.

I flopped down beside Mama, ready for her to drop the bomb.

"Your teacher called this afternoon," she said.

I scratched my hands. They tingled so badly, I wanted to lick them.

"She's concerned about you. Apparently she caught you doodling in class. I told her we would discuss the possibility of finding a tutor."

"Mama, it's like the middle of the night. Can't we talk about this tomorrow?"

But once I heard her words, I knew there was nothing I could do. I leaned against the table, ignoring the tingling that had crawled up my arm.

Mama glared at me with her coffee-isn't-working-anymore face. "She also says that you've been skipping P.E."

"Who cares about P.E.?"

"Well, I care. What is the reason for this?" Mama asked.

I studied the clock above the oven. It flashed "12:00," which I took for a bad sign. I let it blink three times before I spoke.

"Mama, I have something to say." I sucked in a breath. "I hate swimming."

"Fin, you used to love swimming in Lake Champlain."

"Well, this isn't a lake. It's a pool and it smells nasty. I'm probably going to get sick from the germs."

"Honey, it's chlorinated. There aren't any germs."

"It's more than that," I said. No stopping now. "Sometimes I get these thoughts."

Mama frowned. "What sort of thoughts?"

"Like when I'm folding laundry. I'll start worrying about folding the sleeves in a certain order."

Mama stared at the cigarette glowing between her fingers. "What do you mean a certain order?"

"Well, if I'm getting ready for school. I'll be brushing my teeth and then I'll tell myself, if I don't brush a certain number of times, something bad will happen." Mentioning the ritual made me want to count again. I drummed the table three times.

She got quiet. "Are you hearing voices?"

I squeezed my fists. "I'm not crazy."

Mama took my hand. I cupped the other one on top to make it even. She said, "I don't think you're crazy, Fin. Sometimes when you don't get enough sleep, your mind plays tricks on you."

"I'm not imagining things. When it tells me to do something—"

"Who tells you? I thought you didn't hear voices," Mama said.

This wasn't going anywhere. I tried another approach. "Remember when I used to think there were monsters in my room? You would get out the 'monster spray' and banish them."

Mama looked away as though listening to a more interesting conversation someplace else.

"It's not like I believe in monsters anymore. I just worry all the time."

"Worry about what? The divorce?"

"Everything," I said.

Mama grabbed an empty jelly jar on the table and tipped ash into it. "Well, I think we should find someone for you to talk to."

It took me two seconds to figure this out.

"I'm not going to see a shrink," I said. Their offices were full of crazy people. Maybe it was contagious.

"Look, Fin," Mama said. "I don't know what else to do." She ground out her cigarette. No wonder I couldn't breathe. The house was clogged with toxic fumes. I needed to wash my hands, so I stood up to leave. Mama tried to hug me, but I broke away.

"How long have you felt this way?" asked Mama. She sounded worried.

"Ever since we moved, it's been so much worse."

"You miss your father."

I nodded. Whatever.

"You'd rather live in Vermont."

What was I supposed to say? I didn't have to say anything. She didn't want to hear it.

"Look at me when I'm talking to you."

I kept watching the clock. The numbers glowed.

Mama slammed the table. "I told you to look at me."

My head was throbbing. My hands were throbbing.

"Look here."

I peeled my gaze off the clock. I looked Mama straight in the eyes. When I was little, she used to count, "Three, two, one," until I stopped messing around. She never made it to one.

"Why won't you talk to me?" she said.

Why bother? She wouldn't believe me.

"Fin."

"Just leave me alone, okay? You're not getting it. And no stupid doctor is going to get it."

Mama slid her arm around me. "Please," she said. "Help me understand."

Legally Blind

I slouched in my creaking metal chair. The day had just started, and I was already counting the seconds to leave. Sharon Lubbitz had made a big deal about me breathing too loudly or sitting too close. She wiggled my desk, mumbling what she'd do if given a chance.

"What if I shoved that pen in your eye?" Sharon whispered. Her braces glinted.

"Shove a pen in my eye?" I echoed, just loud enough for Ms. Armstrong to hear.

After that, I was moved to a corner desk near the busted window. I didn't consider this a punishment. The desk was clean, a blank canvas.

My new neighbor, Thayer Pinsky, tapped my shoulder a lot.

"Quit it," I whispered.

He grinned. "Don't you like boys?"

"Not if they're like you."

He actually looked hurt.

I kept hearing Sharon's words in my head. *Pen, eye, pen, eye*. They wouldn't stop unless I took action. So I grabbed my pen, the tip sharp as a weapon, and lightly touched my eyelids. This didn't do the trick. I drummed faster.

Ms. Armstrong was watching me. Maybe she had called out a question. She seemed to be waiting for an answer.

Her dirty look sent me over the edge. I combed my lashes with the dagger-tipped pen. My eyes itched like crazy. I rubbed them until the room blurred. Oh, God. I could tell by the awful, papery sensation under my left lid that I had pushed my contact lens where none had gone before.

Panicking, I kneaded my fist into the aching socket. This only made it worse. Tears leaked out of my eyes and splatted on my paper.

"Are you okay?" Thayer asked. He had been in the middle of another rant, telling Ms. Armstrong about some dead rapper, as if she cared. "His lyrics are ill, but his delivery and flow aren't anything special," I heard him say between sniffles. "Some of his tracks got weak-ass punches."

I blinked, rapid-fire. Finally, the contact dribbled out. Where it had landed I couldn't guess. Now I had another problem. I couldn't handle walking around with only one contact. Forget the fact that I couldn't see straight. When I looked forward, a swirling fog hovered in every corner. I covered half my face with my hand. It didn't help.

One contact. Only one contact.

So there was only one thing left to do. Flinching, I pinched the remaining contact from my eye and flicked it on the floor. No use saving it. They were disposable anyway. Mama made me get them last year when I couldn't read the blackboard. I had been losing my sight so slowly, I had no idea. I didn't start out wearing glasses before I got contacts because I didn't know that I needed them. When I popped in the lenses, I remember staring at the trees out the window.

"They have so many leaves," I had said.

Without my contacts, I couldn't see anything. I needed to be two feet from a blackboard that others could read from twenty feet away.

Ms. Armstrong caught me waving. "Do you have a question?"

My mind summoned four hundred possibilities. I narrowed them down to one.

"May I use the restroom?"

The class laughed.

"Loser," I heard Sharon say. I couldn't see her sneer, but I could imagine.

"No more bathroom breaks," Ms. Armstrong said.

"It's an emergency. My contact fell out."

For some reason, this always worked. The line came in handy, even for those who wore glasses.

"For real?" said Thayer's raspy voice. I noticed a boy-shaped blur fumbling in front of me. "I've got good eyes. I'll help you find it."

"No thanks."

"Hey, I don't bite . . . hard," he said.

We hunched on the floor, raking the carpet with our fingernails.

"I didn't know you wore contacts," he said.

"Not on purpose," I told him.

"But you always hold your notes so close."

"What?"

I had to get out of there. I grabbed my bag and scrambled past Thayer, bumping elbows as I cruised down the aisle. Somebody stuck out their foot and I tripped. More giggles as I gathered myself up. I slammed into the door before I found the handle.

Outside, the sunlight burned. My school didn't look anything like the cozy hallways I'd studied on cable. The covered walkways didn't offer any UV protection. Our lockers weren't full-length closets where you could store coats as well as books. Who wore coats? Instead, we got mailbox-size cubes and we had to buy our own locks. If they weren't standard black, the principal would cut them off with a hacksaw. This actually happened when I picked out a hot pink lock, just to seem un-boring.

The school reminded me of a parking garage. Replace the cars with rows of numbered doors and you get the idea. No grassy lawns where I could turn cartwheels or play Ultimate Frisbee (people had laughed when I asked if anyone was into it). Just a few cracked tennis courts and the icy glitter of broken glass. No wonder I considered the bathroom a place of solace.

I stumbled inside the girls' room and headed for the nearest stall. Those stupid girls would take forever. I pictured them outlining their lips, though it looked fake as hell. I could stay in my hiding spot for a while. I was safe as long as I was invisible.

Pressing close to the wall, I made out words. Beneath I love Brandon McCormick (a particularly lush senior who inspired godlike worship) somebody had penciled, Not enough to keep you from vandalizing the bathroom.

And underneath, in puffy little-girl script:

If U luv him, have some class.
Don't write his name where U wipe your ass.

When nobody sees you, it's so much easier to be real.

Think: Nobody knows U R here. Do they really know U?

36

Did I really know them?

There were twenty-three of us in my class. Which of them had decided, "I'll bring a pen to the girls' bathroom and express my deepest feelings"? I scanned the handwriting for clues. Who wrote in all capital letters? Who dotted their *i*'s with hearts? Some of the tags were signed *NERS*, which made me think of "nerve."

My eyes darted around, searching for my name. Apparently, my weirdness wasn't worth mentioning.

Burning clouds, shooting stars, three-eyed unicorns. Everything was cool as long as you didn't take credit for it.

The same concept applied to high school as a whole. For example, if a popular girl like Sharon Lubbitz said, "I like your shoes," it could mean one of the following:

• You're trying too hard.

• You should burn those nasty Chuck Taylors.

• I don't really like your shoes. I'm saying this so you'll turn around and tell me, "Don't mention my feet. They're the size of Ping-Pong paddles. I should really see a plastic surgeon."

That's the way things worked. Somebody paid you a compliment and you pretended it didn't matter. But it did matter. It mattered a lot. Still, if you scored well on a math test, you said, "My brother helped me study." If a boy smiled in your direction, you said, "He needs glasses." If you sang better than everybody at assembly, you said, "That wasn't me." And that's true. It's never you.

Taking credit was like taping a bull's-eye to your back. You were just asking for trouble. Better put yourself down before somebody beats you to it.

NERS broke the rules, signing all her felt-tipped doodles. The bold-faced letters floated beneath the wall's best cartoons. I couldn't figure out if NERS was a name or just extra-long initials. She drew scenes from nature. Not counterfeit palm trees and pink flamingos. She sketched mangrove roots that curled around the doorframe. Manatees hovered like Goodyear blimps.

Who was dumb enough to take credit for their own drawings? NERS made a museum out of the bathroom wall. So what if they drew penises in the manatee's flippers?

I longed to send my own message.

I took out my black Sharpie.

I wrote a single word: WHY?

I stood back and thought, "Not bad."

Now all I had to do was wait.

When I returned to class, Thayer was sitting alone. Everyone else had already left.

"Hey," he said. "I found your contact."

Perfect Rhythm

In orchestra, I counted quarter notes, tapping along without looking at my sheet music. I could always tell when something was off-rhythm. The clashing shapes hit me like paper airplanes. After years of teaching tone-deaf freshmen, Mr. Clemmons didn't need a metronome to keep count. He tapped along with his pencil on the music stand. He had a hearing aid shaped like a lima bean in his left ear. When he got fed up, he turned it off.

Sharon Lubbitz sat next to me, sawing on her violin. She made it her personal duty to remind me of my freakishness. When I didn't turn the page, she lost her place and got flak from Mr. Clemmons, who made the whole class stop in mid-squeak.

"It's her fault," Sharon said. "She can't read music." She glared at me and I quickly looked down at our songbook.

"What?" Mr. Clemmons tilted his good ear toward us. "Is that true, Fin?" he asked.

I shrugged. Of course I could read music.

"Well?" Mr. Clemmons waited.

"I don't need the songbook," I told him. "I can see the notes in my head."

Mr. Clemmons drummed the piano. "Tell me, Fin. What time signature is this?"

I sat there, counting. In my mind, a crowd of numbers raced through the finish line. I told him, "It's in 8/8 time," and he beamed.

"And this?" he said. His chalky hands flew across the keys. You couldn't pay me to touch that dirty piano.

"It's 4/4. Like the highway," I said, my voice sounding trembly.

"The highway?"

The other kids gawked as if I had spoken in Martian.

"The sound of the cars on the highway," I said,

feeling silly. "It's the same beat. One passes every couple seconds."

"How do you know?" he asked.

"Because I counted."

Papers fluttered as the class laughed. Then I heard someone cough and say, "She's got perfect rhythm."

I didn't have to turn around. I saw him looking at me from two rows over. Thayer Pinsky. He was always hanging around the music room, although I'd never seen him play an instrument. Last time I checked, there was no sheet music for beatboxing.

Mr. Clemmons nodded. "Fin, you're one in a million."

A million? In my head, the zeros rolled on and on.

"Does that make her an idiot savant?" Sharon said. "Or just an idiot?"

"Some people are rhythmically impaired," Thayer shot back.

After school ended, Mama was standing in the parking lot. I got in the car and said nothing. Heading north on US-1, I could see that the landscape looked thirsty. Miles of fast-food joints—mostly Pollo Tropicals and Miami Subs—decorated with cardboard pumpkins littered the highway. We zoomed past a gas station selling "homemade" Key lime pie.

"They're not real Key limes," said Mama, "unless they come from Key West."

I cranked down the window so all I heard was the slippery rush of traffic, snatching her sentences and flinging them south. Half dozing, I counted the *ka-thump, ka-thump* of tires on pavement, the Spanish newscasters on the radio.

Mama swerved down a side street. GAS, FOOD, LODGING, said a sign. It sounded like the lyrics to a song. We parked under a palm tree choked with red ribbons. SAY NO TO DRUGS! said a banner on the chain-link fence. Inside the *O*'s were smiley faces.

That's what bugs me about the Sunshine State. Everybody expects you to be happy all the time, like you're living on vacation. But it's not a vacation if you never get to leave.

The shrink's office reminded me of a train, all one story, with narrow windows. Stringy loops of graffiti ballooned across the back wall. A few words extended to the bushes.

The waiting room smelled like cough syrup. Across from me, a girl with poodle bangs kept staring at the television. I leaned to the farthest corner of my chair.

Mama offered me some water. I stared at the paper cup, pictured the germs wiggling around it, and shook my head no.

"Why did you drag me here? I'm not sick," I told Mama. Even as I spoke, I arranged my thoughts in this order: sickness, doctors, medicine. Mama pretended not to hear me.

On the TV, a blond woman jumped out of a sports car. The channel on the cable box was blinking "nineteen." I got up and clicked it to ten.

"Excuse me. I was watching that," said the poodle-haired girl.

I didn't move.

The girl waited for me to change it back. When I didn't, she got out of her seat and clicked it herself. By that time, my brain had latched on to the number nineteen. I kept adding the nine and the one together to make ten. My fingers started tapping, pinkie to thumb, left to right.

"Sit still," Mama hissed.

Nineteen surged in me, looking for a suitable target. I tried to keep from thinking about it. I rose from my chair.

"Fin? What's going on?" she asked.

I bolted out of the waiting room. The receptionist gave me a funny look when I ran past, but I didn't stop until I reached the door. I had to get out of there, away from all those people, breathing my air.

I walked to the car, though I couldn't unlock it.

Mama was there a moment later. We stood in the parking lot, watching the river of cars. I counted three blue sedans in 4/4 time before she spoke to me.

"Dr. Calaban is waiting," she said. "Are you going back inside?"

I didn't have the energy to say no.

Happiness of the Garden Variety

All sunsets are frauds. Don't tell me otherwise. When I stared at the posters blitzed throughout the shrink's waiting room, I got a shorthand glimpse of happy endings. Their horizons dissolved like tissue paper, though I knew the sun doesn't actually "rise" or "set." It's just a figure of speech. Ms. Armstrong says that sunsets contain lithium. That's why it feels good to watch the colors caramelize.

STD? Who, me? read a cartoon-infested pamphlet flopped on the table. *Abstinence or AIDS,* read another, making it sound like a choice between the two. I sat next to Mama, counting to three as I read the letters forward and backward. STDAIDS AIDSSTD I counted letters until they no longer made sense. When I reached thirty, a nice round number, I slid my eyes to the boy in the next seat. He thumbed through a woman's magazine and opened a spread called: *Your lifetime horoscope. Where you will be in ten, twenty, thirty years.* I was more concerned about the next five minutes. A soft, blond girl in the hallway kept sneezing into the same tissue. The office was probably crawling with germs. I needed to wash my hands.

"Fin," said Mama. "The lady is speaking to you."

I looked up.

"Frances?" said the receptionist. I cringed at the old-fashioned, little-girl sound of my name. "You've never been counseled before?" Her sentences had an upward-tilting quality that made me grit my teeth.

She gave me a smile and a test, the sort where you scribble in the bubbles. My answers looked wrong, no matter what I wrote. *Sometimes, never, or often* were my only choices. *Sometimes do you feel guilty without explanation? Do you never think things will go right? How often do you feel sad, blue, or down in the dumps?* It didn't seem fair, asking those kinds of questions. Anyone could jot *sometimes* and sound as if their brain had gone haywire.

"Have you lost interest in things you once enjoyed?" the test prodded, almost daring me to say no. My interests changed on a constant basis. I couldn't even listen to a new CD without getting sick of it within a week.

"Do you wonder HOW you could commit suicide?" asked the next question. Maybe I was wrong, but I couldn't help believing that everyone had thought about killing themselves, if only out of curiosity. Of course I had wondered about it. At least, if I planned my death, I could have some control over things, like what dress I'd be wearing and how my hair would be arranged. I didn't really consider how I'd attempt it (the movies always made it look so messy, especially when it involved slicing your wrists), but I liked to imagine my parents reading my good-bye letter.

"We were too hard on her," Mama would say, adjusting my barrettes.

"I should've spent more time with her," Dad would chime in.

"Have you done this before?" I heard a voice call out.

I lifted my gaze from the test. The voice belonged to a malnourished-looking boy who was slurping a can of Iron Beer, a Cuban soda that could've been mistaken for booze. He flopped down on the sofa next to me. His skin was pale, almost see-through. Then he coughed once, twice, and I recognized him.

"Are you a regular?" Thayer asked, rubbing his nose.

"Regular what?"

"Some of the freaks here are, like, regulars. They become addicted, you know. I'm just in for a check-up. My doctor makes me come here every month."

I took a sudden interest in the television.

"Frances, dear," said the receptionist, "did you finish already?" She squinted at the test, then at me, as though connecting the two. Maybe she was try-ing to guess if I cheated. Could you cheat on these kinds of tests?

While stuck in the magazine-infested waiting room, making shorthand assumptions about my fel-low mental patients, it crossed my mind that psychi-atrists get paid for the same service.

"Thayer Pinsky," said the receptionist, beaming at the boy beside me. "Good afternoon."

He gave her a military-style salute. A regular, I suspected.

"So you're depressed, huh?" Thayer whispered to me. "Aren't we all."

I stroked my chair like a guitar. If the boy saw me do it, he didn't say anything. I was trapped, with the receptionist in front and the pale boy beside me.

"Young lady?" the receptionist called out.

I chewed a hangnail on my pinkie. I was thinking about the phrase "young lady" and how much I hated it.

Mama said the receptionist had called my name again. Dr. Calaban didn't have all day.

I felt people staring—crazy kids and their parents—but I couldn't budge until the third time she called me. Thayer smirked. He probably thought I was being rebellious. As I stood up, he saluted me. How pathetic. My one moment of coolness came in a loony bin.

Mama squeezed my hand.

"Good luck," she said.

I squeezed back twice.

Dr. Calaban was waiting in her office. Contrary to my imagination, it lacked a couch. A box of "ultra-comfort" Kleenex and a coffee mug that read, *What? Me Worry?* crowded her cluttered desk. Behind it sat Dr. Calaban—a spidery woman in a long hippy-dippy skirt. Her skin glowed dark as hardwood floors. I couldn't take my eyes off her Afro-puffed curls, almost tamed under a sparkly scarf.

"Frances," she said. Her accent was musical, pouring out in a silky ribbon. "I'm Dr. Calaban. What brings you here?"

"Oh, the usual," I said. The air conditioner hummed so loud, I turned it off without asking.

"Perhaps you could be more specific?"

"I can't . . . I mean, no. Not really."

I studied her bracelet. A chain of tiny yellow skulls clattered like teeth around her wrist. She caught my stare.

"My guru gave this to me," she said, as if that explained everything.

I lowered my gaze to a metal bowl with sea-weedy plants springing out of it. On the wall behind Dr. Calaban was a blue and red banner with a coat of arms—swords and cannons pointed toward a palm tree. I wanted to snatch it off the wall and hang it in my room.

"That's the Haitian national flag," she said. "One of many we've had over the years."

"Huh," I said. That explained the musical accent.

"I took a look at your test," she said.

I tried to make a joke. "Did I pass or fail?"

"It's not that kind of test," she said. "Have you been feeling like this for a while?"

"Feeling like what?"

"Tired or sad."

"Who doesn't?" I said.

Dr. Calaban let out a long sigh. "Have you been experiencing any thoughts of suicide?"

I shrugged. "Once in a while. Doesn't everybody?"

Dr. Calaban wasn't even paying attention. She was flipping through papers. I couldn't get over it.

Nobody was listening, not even the stupid lady doctor. That was the end of my patience. I was so tired, I started shaking.

Dr. Calaban handed me a Kleenex.

The room shimmered. I wiped my eyes.

"Frances, can you explain why you're crying?"

No, I couldn't.

God, I hated crying in public. Especially in this Lysol atmosphere. The more I tried to stop, the worse it got. I started counting backward inside my head, *Ten, nine, eight.* But it didn't chill me out. I'd need to switch the order around. The pattern had an expiration date, like gum that had lost its flavor.

"It's okay. I always cry for no reason."

Dr. Calaban nodded like a fortune-teller. She didn't say anything.

"I thought we were supposed to be talking about stuff," I said.

"What would you like to talk about?"

I drew stars with one finger into my fist, around and around.

Dr. Calaban said, "Do you realize that you've

been playing with your hands since you first sat down?"

"Playing with my hands?" I gripped the chair legs, just to stop fidgeting.

"Do you have a lot of nervous habits, Frances?" she asked.

"I wouldn't call them habits," I said.

"Then what would you call them?" she asked.

"Just these things that I do. They don't mean anything," I said, squeezing the chair legs three times, hoping she didn't notice.

Her voice drifted away. She gave me a card with a date and time scrawled on it.

"I look forward to speaking further with you, Frances," she said, as if inviting me to a party.

I grabbed my book bag and banged into one of Dr. Calaban's potted plants. It crashed at her feet, an African violet encased in a clump of veiny dirt. I tried to scoop it back into the plastic container. The price tag was still attached. Two dollars, ninety-five cents.

"Sorry," I said, although I wasn't.

"About time I bought a new pot. You'd be

surprised how fast they grow." She smiled.

Was she trying to make a joke? If so, I wasn't laughing.

In the waiting room, Dr. Calaban shook Mama's hand. I watched them talk, but I couldn't concentrate. I pictured Dr. Calaban at her desk, scribbling notes on a memo pad. Would I recognize this portrait of myself?

"I'm setting up regular appointments," said the receptionist. Her glasses dangled so low on her beaky nose, they seemed in danger of falling off. She gave me a preprinted card, the kind I might've used to memorize the multiplication tables. The other side featured a time (9 a.m.) and Dr. Calaban's bold-faced name. Why would she schedule an appointment during class? Not that I was complaining.

"So Fridays are good for you?"

I gave a little shrug.

The receptionist said, "Take care, Frances," as if we had known each other for years. I scanned the room for Thayer, but he had already gone. I tried to imagine him in Dr. Calaban's office, slouched in the same chair, still warm from where I sat.

Outside the air felt minty. It smelled like a freshly cut football field. I listened to an elementary school, as heard from a distance. I could tell it was dismissal time, judging by the amount of shrieking and whistle-blowing taking place between cheers. I remembered sitting on our P.E. field back in Vermont, plucking warm handfuls of grass—the soft, spongy variety, not the hypergreen, itchy stuff that felt like Astroturf in our Florida backyard. Both were good for making music. I could play a blade of grass like a flute. If I mentioned something like this to Dr. Calaban, she wouldn't get it. To her, I was just another crazy patient, a page from one of her books. I had to talk to her in a way that made sense. I had to be careful not to reveal too much.

The Glowing Pickle

When I snuck in late to earth science the next morning, Thayer was already there, doodling away. The only seat left was the wobbly one. Ms. Armstrong was wasting time, taking attendance. She refused to mark me present.

"There's no excuse for being this late," she said.

No fair. I glanced at the periodic table of elements on the wall above Ms. Armstrong's head, arranged in rows—oxygen, carbon, hydrogen, nitrogen, and so on. Something about the parade of invisible solids, liquids, and gases depressed me. They were always changing, while I was doomed to sit at my desk.

We read about exploding stars and black holes, but it all seemed so distant. Even though I knew these books were giving scientific information, it felt like a fantasy to me. I didn't think I could ever be part of the universe in our books.

My neck became sore during class. When I rested my chin on the desk, Ms. Armstrong called it "sleeping" and yelled at me.

Thayer tapped my shoulder.

"Your shoelace is untied," he whispered.

Before I could stop him, he double-knotted my laces.

"It's safer that way."

His voice seemed extra soft.

Even the kids from my neighborhood didn't talk to me in class. I ignored him and chewed my fingers.

After class, Ms. Armstrong pulled me aside.

"We need to talk about your performance so far." Her voice reminded me of a phone operator's. "You're a smart girl. But I think you can do better. I suspect you've been distracted from your work. It's okay to talk about it. Nothing you tell me will go beyond this room."

I kept thinking about that phrase, "beyond this

room." There was so much hidden inside the room—the tennis ball that had socked the window like a comet, the missing pieces of her son's photograph (a casualty of the P.E. incident, or so she believed) tucked inside my pencil box.

Somebody knocked on the door. Ms. Armstrong grabbed it.

"Yes?" she said, making it a question. "Yes? Yes?"

When she wasn't looking, I stuck out my tongue. Three times.

She jotted something on her hand. What sort of teacher didn't carry a notepad?

Watching Ms. Armstrong scribble on her skin, I got a terrible itching for antibacterial soap.

"I need to use the restroom," I said.

Ms. Armstrong wasn't buying it. "You were late for class."

I nodded three twice.

"Why don't I come with you?" she said, opening the door.

We walked to the bathroom together. Sharon Lubbitz and her followers were there, ripping up magazines and rubbing the perfume samples on their arms. Just smelling them made me nervous, so I flipped the lights on and off three times. They must've told Ms. Armstrong, because she went in after me. She dragged me outside.

"It costs more to flip the switch on and off," she said, "than to leave it on."

"No, it doesn't," said Thayer Pinsky, who had been watching from his usual detention spot on the graffiti-infested bench in the breezeway. "I've checked."

Ms. Armstrong blinked. "Excuse me?"

"I turned my bedroom light on and off for a few minutes and checked the meter."

The girls made faces at him but said nothing. I wanted to mention that I had tried the same experiment last summer, but as I opened my mouth, Thayer looked at me hard. All I could hear was slithery laughter in the parking lot, the baseball team swearing behind their pickup trucks.

Thayer Pinsky was still talking about energy. "Why don't we ever do anything fun in class? At my old school, we used to have a kick-ass science fair."

Ms. Armstrong warned Thayer about using the

word "ass," but he continued his story.

"So everybody used to do the dumbest things like weather balloons or baking soda volcanoes or absorbent cat litter. My science teacher's name was Ms. Veronna. I called her Ms. Piranha. She gave me major attitude."

I didn't doubt it.

"Here's what happened." Thayer talked with the speed of a machine gun. "Miss Piranha says, 'Where's your project, Thayer?' And I go, 'It's the glowing pickle,' and I get up and walk to the front. And I tell her how everything in the world is made of atoms, including us. Even though I wouldn't mind being a boulder or an oak tree, I got stuck with people atoms."

"Are you sure about that?" said Sharon. But he kept rolling.

"So the Piranha can't figure out how I made the pickle glow. Basically, it worked like someone frying in the electric chair."

"That's enough," said Ms. Armstrong.

"If I get suspended again, my mom says she's sending me to military school." He snorted. "That's what she thinks. I'll just run away to New York and stay with my gram. She's mad cool. Like, on the B train, she'll tell me when to look out the window and see these dope-ass tunnels where all the subway writers went underground."

"That kid is so weird," said Sharon, as if he wasn't even there.

When Thayer ran out of words, I ducked in the bathroom. I huddled in the stall while Ms. Armstrong waited. Thayer was so much himself. He buzzed like neon, oblivious.

O	C	T	O	B	E	R
15	3	20	15	2	5	18

Balancing

Dr. Calaban had decided that I suffered from a chemical imbalance.

She let out a sigh. "There are two types of clinical depression: seasonal affective disorder, which relates to the time of the year, and dysthymia, which is identified by hopeless feelings."

One month, three meals, two types.

"I'd like to try medication in conjunction with psychotherapy," she said.

"Medication for what?" I shook my head. "I don't want to take medication. That stuff can have major side effects."

"Well, 'major' is a strong word. Think of it this way. If you were sick, you'd go to a doctor and he or she would prescribe something to make you feel better. This is the same thing."

"But I'm not sick!"

She wrote down a prescription, just like a medical doctor. It had my name on it, along with the word "Paxil."

"There are many different reasons that a person may feel anxious or depressed," she explained. "Depression may be caused by a neurochemical disorder. One thing that many patients have in common is a low level of serotonin, the 'happy chemical' in the brain."

"So my 'happy chemicals' are low?"

"Think of it this way. Serotonin reuptake inhibitors such as Paxil increase serotonin and help the brain communicate."

It was official. My brain, like people on daytime talk shows, was having communication problems.

Dr. Calaban explained that it would take a few weeks for the Paxil to work. I was almost disappointed. I couldn't wait any longer. And what if it didn't work at all? Or worse—what if it changed me into someone else, a robot blissed out on artificial emotions?

Mama didn't seem convinced. She took Dr. Calaban's prescription and crumpled it in her purse.

Why was Mama so ballistic over the medication, especially after dragging me to a shrink? Why would she sabotage my chance to get help? I had my own ideas. This was the woman who wouldn't buy lunch meat because it was laced with cancer-causing nitrates. I grew up in a house without sugared cereal or soda. When I got sick, she always told me to take more vitamins. When I was sad, she said the same thing.

I had a feeling that my problem was bigger than vitamin C.

Gossip

Days passed and NERS didn't write. PLEASE, I scribbled again and again. ANSWER.

Still nothing.

On Monday, I stood guard near the girls' restroom, watching couples lean against lockers. Sharon was sucking face with her latest conquest. I saw them from the side: Sharon's firm, bright mouth, and the boy's stubbled chin, dotted with toilet paper. They kissed and kissed as if trying to prove something. Sharon's hands were all over the place. She tugged his jacket. The boy stumbled. I watched them slink away, holding hands and staring in opposite directions.

How could someone so mean score a boyfriend?

I pushed the door open.

At the sink, Sharon's disciples, Colleen and

Jessica, were smudging blush on the apples of their cheeks. I thought about leaving, but I had to see if NERS had answered me.

"Hi," I said, sliding around them.

The girls didn't glance at me. They giggled as though I had told a joke.

I ducked inside the handicap stall. As usual, the others were out of order.

H. K. still loved C. J. forever and Casey sucked four-letter words. But there, in black Sharpie, beneath WHY? were the words:

WHY NOT?

The letters had dripped and faded. I leaned forward and sniffed their faint, mediciney stink.

"Can you believe that skank? She thinks she's all that." Colleen's mosquito-thin voice grated in my ear.

I inched backward, though nobody could see me.

"She's nothing but a chickenhead," Jessica chimed in.

"I can honestly say that Sharon needs to disappear," said Colleen.

Could this be happening? Sharon, the alpha female, was getting trashed by her so-called buds.

"I'm not trying to be a hater," Colleen said. "I mean, I like her most of the time. But there are definitely better-looking girls out there."

"And she has this fake shake-and-bake tan."

"And what's up with the dude that she's macking on? He shaves his eyebrows so he won't look so Latino."

"Nasty."

"Hold on," Colleen said. "I need to pee really bad."

I nibbled a hangnail. No way could I sneak out without snagging more attention. Not after that gabfest. The girls had really mastered the art of fakery. For no reason, a best friend could turn on you. If boys had a problem, they just punched each other out. And weirdoes like Thayer didn't belong in any category. They floated under the radar.

"Don't take all day." Amber pounded on the stall. "I'm, like, going to explode in ten seconds."

My mind clung to the digit.

"Make that nine," she added.

God, I hated that number. It had this less-than-perfect aura about it. Not to mention, when you turned it upside down, it morphed into six.

"Get a move on, stupid."

I stared at the wall. I needed to whisk the nines out of my brain, so I doodled a wreath of them.

Colleen lost it. She kicked the stall with such force, the lock slipped out of place. I jammed it back again. I didn't want to deal, so I kept drawing. With my luck, she wouldn't go away.

"I know it's you, Frances. God. What a freak."

Better than being a slut, I wanted to say. Why didn't I just spit it out? She wore tight clothes— microminis, low-rise jeans. She hid nothing.

"Why don't you just kill yourself?" she said.

I needed to tune out.

I drew nine chains of nine. After that, I was almost at peace. Then I looked down and saw Colleen's face near my feet.

My pen hit the floor and rolled.

"You're going to be in so much trouble," she told me.

"No, I'm not," I managed to squeak. "Because if you rat on me, I'll tell Sharon what you said about her."

Colleen was still hanging upside down, trying to peer inside the stall.

"You wouldn't."

"I would."

Her face disappeared.

"Whatever," she said.

The door creaked and banged shut.

The words on the wall had given me special powers.

I took a deep breath and wrote, WHO?

The next day, NERS responded with, WHO DO U BELIEVE IN?

On Friday, I wrote, WHAT?

Later that afternoon, NERS scribbled, WHAT U SCARED 4?

But our match ended the morning I wrote, WHEN? and NERS asked, WHEN CAN WE MEET?

I spread my left hand wide enough to outline it with a Bic pen (but not so wide that it resembled a manatee). The pen wobbled and skittered over the wall's gum-caked grooves. Then I added:

ELEMENTARY PLAYGROUND. IN 7 DAYS. 12 NOON.

Before I left, I thought of one last thing.

TRACE YOUR HAND ON THE WALL, I wrote.

Guinea Pig Girl

On Saturday morning, Mama was digging in the dirt, pretending to "garden." Verb form of a noun. Not that we had a garden. Not in Florida, where the dirt is choked with rock.

Mama put me to work, washing shells in a plant saucer. The shells were stuffed with dead acorns, along with unidentifiable chunks of mulch. I was bringing them back to life. Each shell held a ghost, the spirit of sea-things past.

"Where are these from?" I asked.

"Don't you remember?" Mama said. "Sanibel Island. You had fun collecting them."

I remembered the trip but not the shells. Just my parents yelling.

My parents had two ways of fighting. In the first round, they hollered. Dad always won because his lungs were bigger. Mama always won the second round. She could ignore Dad for days. And since words were his favorite weapon, he didn't have a chance.

Dad worked for a giant ad agency, making up sentences he called "copy." If you've ever read the back of a cereal box, it's possible Dad wrote the crap about starting your day with a smile. He kept notebooks full of stupid phrases like "clusters of wholesome, hearty bran" and "plenty of plump, juicy raisins and real oats in every low-fat serving."

It's true. Dad ate cereal with little hearts on the box.

When the ad agency landed another "good for your heart, lower your cholesterol" campaign, they grew so big, they moved a branch south. At first, Dad was psyched. Although he mostly wrote about crunchy granola at home, he'd grown sick of driving back and forth to New York for meetings.

Mama couldn't wait to ditch Vermont. She had bought a Sun Box lamp to banish the winter blues. But once we moved to Miami, we didn't act like the unstoppable Nash trio anymore. Dad was "busting his hump" round the clock. Mornings, he left with a briefcase, and at night he collapsed on the couch.

He didn't talk much about his ad pitches. "Top secret," he'd say, as if Mama and I were spies. He'd crack open a Heineken without saying a word.

Mama would hide in the kitchen, scrubbing pots. She rinsed them over and over again, though she'd spent a lot of money on a new dishwasher. She kept her hands busy, rinsing and scrubbing, as if that would make things right.

The trip to Sanibel Island was Mama's bright idea. Dad wasn't too thrilled. He lugged his laptop to the hotel and passed the week squinting and barking at it.

That's when I got on bad terms with the ocean. I hated the aquarium taste of the water and the way it stung my eyes. It dried into a salty crust and knotted my ponytail so tight, I cut the tangles out with scissors.

I sat in the itchy sand, watching seagulls rip a fast-food wrapper apart. The pound, pound, pounding of the Gulf's pulse jangled my nerves. I needed a pause button. Or a pair of earplugs.

My parents were at each other's throats. After the shouting, they waged a creepy battle without sound.

Kids say there's nothing sadder than hearing your parents fight. But at that point, I would've given anything for a little screaming and yelling. It was so much worse when they didn't care enough to argue.

Dad holed up in our room, clacking away on his PowerBook. Mama paced back and forth on the beach, collecting shells, as if she could tidy up the entire coast.

The space in my head needed filling, so I started cramming it with numbers. Safe, solid numbers, like fives and tens, that stood on their own, no explanation required. Words just cluttered my thoughts. The beach kept time with my inner metronome, a sound that went on and on, whether I was there to hear it or not.

I turned off the garden hose and looked at Mama. Even the constellations of moles on her upper arm seemed unfamiliar. I stared at the cigarette glowing between her fingers. "It's a little early for a smoke, don't you think?"

"Two is my limit."

I raised an eyebrow.

"Make that two-thirty in the afternoon," she said.

Mama waited for me to laugh. When I didn't, she said, "Don't get on my case."

She was shoveling handfuls of wet dirt and rotten leaves into a garbage can. I was supposed to be raking, but instead, I sat there, wondering how to reach her. I closed my eyes.

"The shrink wants me to take medication," I said.

I hated the idea of taking pills. More than that, I hated the idea of taking pills for something that I should handle on my own.

Mama said, "I saw your prescription. Paxil is heavy stuff, Fin. It's been linked to suicide. I saw it on the news."

I said, "Something has messed up my head." For some reason, I couldn't stand the word "depression."

Mama found an empty jelly jar on the railing and tipped ash into it. "There is absolutely nothing wrong with your head, Fin."

"How do you know?" I asked.

Mama tilted her head. She peered through the

shadow of her baseball cap.

"Some people think medication can fix anything." I watched her exhaling smoke. "Yet this country tells us to 'say no to drugs.'"

"It's not a drug. It's medication," I said.

"Antidepressants are terribly overprescribed," she said. "They're giving that stuff out like candy these days."

First Mama pushed me to see a doctor. Now she was contradicting herself. I couldn't stand listening to her anymore.

"I didn't ask to see Dr. Calaban. It was your big idea."

"Medication is for sick people," she said. "My daughter is not sick."

I thought about what Dr. Calaban had decided, that I suffered from a chemical imbalance. Did this explain why I worried so much? Or why I needed to wash my hands until they bled? Or why numbers floated through my mind when I heard music? Would that go away if I took medication?

"The pharmaceutical bigwigs are worse than the tobacco industry when it comes to marketing this stuff to kids." Mama's voice dropped to a croak. "Their only goal is to get kids hooked so they pop pills for the rest of their lives."

"Hold on. I haven't decided if I want to try it yet."

"I refuse to let my daughter be a guinea pig."

"It's not like I'm the first person to use anti-depressants."

"And where is the money going to come from?"

"Mama, you work for an insurance company. You know this stuff. Dr. Calaban said we could look into it."

I tried to focus on what Mama was saying. Something about Dad's company.

"I don't think they're going to cover it," she said.

What did Mama know anyway? She wasn't a doctor.

I threw the shells in the garbage. That's where I found my prescription, wet with coffee grounds. I took it out and stuffed it in my pocket. Then I scrubbed my hands under the hose until they were scraped clean.

They Have No Idea

I had forged Mama's signature, biked to the drug-store, and gave it to the white-coated woman behind the counter. For an hour, I wandered the aisles. I pushed buttons on the blood pressure monitor. I hung around the photo department. An old man had taken pictures of nothing except his Dalmatian puppies. It must get pretty boring developing snapshots of other people's happy occasions, all those proms and birthday parties.

Back at the prescription counter, I handed the lady pharmacist a few wadded-up twenties, the last of my birthday money, and bought the pills. On the bottle was my name and the letters *RX*, which I juggled back and forth, counting one two, one two. *XR RX XR RX*. Like holding the letters up to a mirror and seeing them stretch into infinity.

I walked to an abandoned house at the end of our street. The owners, a couple of shotgun-toting hippies, had left after Hurricane Andrew and never came back.

I stared at the empty house. When I shook the door, it didn't budge. Neither did the windows, still boarded shut against hurricanes. I tried the other side. A sheet of plywood dangled from a broken window. I pushed it back and scrambled inside.

I stepped down, my flip-flops crunching invisible things. Everything was left eerily in place, just before they fled the hurricane.

Sitting cross-legged on the floor, I opened my backpack and pulled out the prescription. I took out a pink pill. I studied the word, "Paxil," stamped on one side. "Pax," a word from a dead language. It meant peace. At that moment, I needed all the peace I could get. I washed it down with a can of warm soda from my backpack and waited for something to happen. Maybe I would lose whatever made me different from everyone else. I couldn't decide if I liked the idea.

I hid the pills under a sofa cushion, then climbed out the broken window.

The counting didn't stop. I counted windows in my bedroom, chairs at the dining-room table, lights in the bathroom. The list went on and on. I would be in the middle of counting something and realize, *Oh, I'm counting again.*

Mama was counting too. She counted how much time I spent in the bathtub. If I didn't finish in fifteen minutes, she would knock on the door.

"You're just trying to get attention," she would say. As if wanting her attention was a bad thing.

All she did was smoke cigarettes and watch the Weather Channel like a robot. She'd yell at me, then melt whenever she picked up the phone and asked people to buy insurance.

If I talked about trying medication, she would fly into a rage.

"Everybody has bad days. My life isn't fun either. You never think about anyone but yourself." This is what Mama would say.

I needed someone to talk to. So I called Dad at

work. Although he still lived in Florida, it felt like he existed in another dimension. He had even started dating. I hadn't met her yet. I wasn't exactly looking forward to it.

Dad's voice floated out of the receiver.

"Hello, grasshopper," he said.

"Hey, are you busy?"

I could hear voices in the background, cabinets slamming.

"It's a little hectic around here. Hold on."

I waited. When he came back, I cleared my throat. "I haven't been feeling well lately."

Dad's volume rose a notch. "What's wrong? Are you sick?"

"My doctor wants me to take this medicine. And I'm afraid it will make me different."

"What do you mean 'different'? What kind of medicine?"

I shrugged. There were so many kinds of antidepressants and, for a second, I had forgotten its name.

"Have you spoken to your mother about this?"

"Yeah. She doesn't want to pay for it."

A low blow. But I had to do something.

"Put her on the phone," he said.

"She's not around right now."

"Frances, this really isn't a good time. I've got a major deadline."

"Well, *bon chance*."

"What?"

"That's French for good luck."

"Listen," he said. "I'm here if you need to talk. We'll go out for dinner soon with Yara, okay? Call me at home."

Yara was Dad's new girlfriend. How could I talk with her around?

Somewhere outside, a plane cruised seven miles above the earth. The lawnmower man was making parallelograms out of the grass. I realized I had nothing more to say.

Awake Still

For weeks, I'd been riding back and forth to the empty house, taking Paxil before bed. Dr. Calaban thought I could sleep off any side effects— the headaches and nausea. Instead, I didn't sleep at all. I heard noises that weren't real, like electronic doorbells. When I moved my head, their rhythm picked up speed.

On Saturday, I hid under the covers, but Mama kept banging on my door, saying we should talk. I thought she must have figured out about the Paxil. But how could she know unless the pharmacy called or something? So I rehearsed this speech about how I was almost fifteen and I could make my own decisions.

I needed to do something with my room. On

the wall was a patch-eyed pirate's head carved from a coconut. I could feel it gawking at me. I flopped on my back and stared at the ceiling fan, whirling and churning above like a blender. I used to pin a million things up in my room back in Vermont. Not posters of stupid bands or supermodels. More like dried maple leaves I found while taking a walk. Or this amazing skeleton of a squirrel. I even made a throne of Popsicle sticks for him. Mama called it disgusting. I called it art.

Here, the concrete ruined all attempts at decorating. Besides, Mama wouldn't let me glue stuff on the walls. So I had to think of something new. I tried doodling in my sketchpad, but nothing came out right. I hadn't drawn anything serious in a long time.

I got up and opened the window. *Whoosh* went the cars like drag racers, so noisy compared to my old neighborhood. I thought about where the drivers were rolling and wished they'd take me along. Then I fell asleep and thought about nothing at all.

Mama barged in and turned on the lights.

"This place is a pig sty," she said.

"So what?" I said. "I like it that way."

Mama was having another cleaning fit.

"What's all this junk?" she said, dragging out my bottle-cap collection.

"It's my crap."

"Don't use that word in front of me, young lady."

We sat there in silence. I felt sorry for Mama. She didn't know I was on Paxil or that I tapped a light switch for her, exactly the same way, every night. She didn't know anything about my life. She seemed so pitiful sitting there, picking up my bottle caps.

Every so often, an electric zap would buzz behind my eyes. I had the same out-of-body sensation I got with the flu. I couldn't sleep but never really woke up.

"Go outside. You're making me crazy," said Mama.

For me, it was the other way around.

I slammed the screen door so hard, it rattled. The humidity squeezed all the air out of me. Next door, the neighbor's twin boys were playing in their pool. Their toys floated iceberg-style: tons of crayon-colored foam sticks called "noodles," a couple of pseudo–Native American canoes painted with wigwams.

The boys chattered in Spanish. They waved. I waved back. For a minute, I almost asked if I could join them. Their house was another McMansion. Their treeless yard was surrounded by a gleaming metal fence. On their telephone wire, a pair of shoes dangled, left over like bones on a plate after a meal.

I crossed the street, jogged a few blocks to the park, and watched the little kids play on the exercise bars. I tried to picture them grown up, with boring jobs like Mama's, selling insurance over the phone. Then I almost crashed into two skater boys. They looked at me and I jumped.

"Yo, shortie. Where you headed?" said the first boy. He was wearing a skully cap and a chain belt.

"I don't know," I said.

"You don't?" he asked.

The other boy laughed. It was Thayer. He had

leaves in his dreadlocks and splotches all over his hands. He was actually taller than me.

They were smoking weed and scribbling graffiti on the wall. Huge, puffed-up letters. Not spray paint. Something thicker. Like shoe polish.

"She's gonna narc on us," said the first boy.

Thayer shrugged. "Just chill, man. She won't."

"How can you tell?"

"Because," he said. "I know her."

He stood near me, much closer than was necessary. I could smell ashes on his breath. Thayer put his splotchy palm on me. I almost did the same to him, just to make it even in my mind. Something held me back. His hand stayed put, getting warmer, as if pulling me to him. Then he and the other kid took off on their skateboards.

I touched my shoulder three times. It was still warm.

Protected Species

I was living the life of a junkie. The side effects of swallowing Paxil had started right away. Sunlight hit me like noise, which only made the headaches worse.

For weeks, my dopey, drugged existence was making it impossible to concentrate on school, and my stomach was worse. I had grown used to my headaches, those brain zaps like the sizzle of a nine-volt battery behind my eyes. But I couldn't take the ringing in my head. It hurt to turn my eyes. Aspirin helped a little, but the headache never left.

At school, I felt okay until P.E. We were going to swim laps around the pool while Coach Kiki filed her nails near the diving board. No way was I going to puke in front of Sharon Lubbitz and her personality-impaired clones. Besides. I had other plans. This was the day I would meet NERS.

Maybe NERS was already looking for me on the elementary school playground. Could I wait another forty-five minutes? My stomach flip-flopped.

The coach thought I was faking. Maybe I didn't look as deathlike as I felt. She raised one overly plucked eyebrow and told me to "suck it up" unless I wanted to see the principal. Since I was already in enough trouble, between my miserable grades and countless lunch detentions for doodling in class, I dipped my toe in the shallow end.

I felt the whoosh of air before I smacked the ground. Afterward, I saw the scummy undersides of the bleachers. The pool throbbed.

"Give her some air," said the coach in a quivery voice.

She told me to sit with my head lodged between my knees. I heard Sharon Lubbitz say, "She's faking."

The coach asked, "Can you walk to the nurse?"

I blinked twice, a telegraph for yes.

In the private recovery room, I leaned back on

the cot and considered all the things to count, from the tongue depressors jutting out of a glass jar to the galaxy of pressure points swirling around a yoga poster.

Nurse What's-Her-Name slapped an ice pack on me. I just needed to lie down. She asked a lot of dumb questions: Do you have any bleeding tendencies? Difficulty sleeping? Are you taking any prescriptions?

"No," I lied.

When I asked for an aspirin, she said, "I'm not allowed to give out medication."

"But it's just aspirin. What if I took some from your purse?"

"Do you want to see me get fired?" she asked, yanking the curtain shut.

Dr. Calaban could dish out mind-altering drugs, but the school nurse couldn't give me an aspirin.

I sat with the dripping ice pack, counting while I thought about busting out of there. The whole idea of meeting NERS was shooting darts through my stomach. She could've been anyone—a wacked-out painter who took a job as a janitor. Or a prepubescent genius who would beat me at chess.

The curtain slid back. There was the nurse, blinking at me.

"I heard you," the nurse said. She had a lipstick stain on one of her front teeth. "You were counting. Over and over again."

I looked out the window. I saw boys shooting imaginary guns at each other. My head sizzled. I needed to keep counting.

"Answer me," the nurse said.

I counted to three. Somehow it didn't feel right.

The nurse watched my fingers tapping.

"Frances," the nurse said. "How long have you been doing that?"

She grabbed my hand.

"How long?"

"A few minutes," I said.

This wasn't the right answer. "Were you counting out loud? Or in your head?"

My blood pumped. "I'm not crazy," I said, scooting back. The crinkly sheets on the cot smelled like dust and germs. I was clocking my heartbeats, wondering if they would stop.

"I'm calling your mother," she said.

"Fine. She's not home." I hopped off the cot and headed for the door. Before I could open it, the nurse snagged my arm. Her grip surprised me.

"Let go," I said, jerking away.

I wrestled out of her death-claw grasp and bolted outside. I didn't know where I was running. The elementary school playground seemed like the safest place.

I saw a boy hunched on the swings. There was something familiar about his punky sneakers, holes blasted into the sides from doing flip tricks, ollies, or whatever they're called. This was all I could detect of his identity. If I stared long enough, he would talk to me. Sure enough, his eyes tilted up, turning clear for a moment. He coughed. Thayer.

"I'm collecting audio evidence," he said. He showed me his tape recorder.

I stared. "No kidding."

I had seen the tape recorder in class, assumed it was a lazy student's method of note taking. But when Thayer played back the tape, I heard the relentless thump of the school's vending machine, wind muttering in the hallway, the metallic clang of a locker. On tape, these noises sounded like an alien language. They were all in 4/4 time.

His splotchy hands were covered in marker stains.

"You're NERS," I said. Four letters. One boy.

Thayer bowed. He looked like a homeless kid. The cuffs of his ratty jeans were tucked into his sneakers, the mesh tongues flapping over the cuffs. His dirt-caked sweatshirt was ten sizes too big. Not to mention, it was way too hot outside.

I tried to picture him in the girls' bathroom, sketching undersea murals with felt-tipped markers. I checked out his hands. They were swarming with ink.

"What exactly does NERS mean?" I asked.

He shrugged. "Why does everything have to mean something? It sounds fast and it's easy to write, in case the cops show up. So now I've got a question for you."

"Okay." I waited.

"You didn't answer," he said.

"What?"

"I asked if you wanted a bite." He held up a half-eaten Moon Pie.

"Well, I didn't hear you," I said.

"That's because I said it inside my head."

"You mean, like, psychically?"

His smile was an explosion of pink gums. "So you did hear me!"

Geez, this boy was odd. He motioned to the swing beside him. I thought about running. Instead, I eased myself into it.

Thayer grinned. "You don't seem like the type to cut class," he said.

"Is that what you're doing?"

He didn't answer. "Let's take a walk."

"Where?"

"Anywhere."

Thayer jumped off the swing. He was smiling at me.

"I don't have time for this," I told him.

"Time is a human invention," he said. "There is no such thing. Look at the stars. It takes millions of years before their light reaches earth. By then, they could already be gone. No use wishing on them."

We walked past the principal's office and the gum-caked water fountains, endlessly gushing l'eau du tap. We passed through empty halls, the basketball court, and a barren row of lockers.

"Where is everybody?" I nibbled my thumbnail.

"Teacher's prep day," Thayer said. "We get out early."

"Oh. Right." I giggled. If we had only a half day of school, why was Thayer still hanging around? I was so busy chewing on this question, I didn't even notice that my headache was gone.

He grabbed my hand. "I want to show you something."

I looked at Thayer's ink-smeared fingers. He might have been crazy, but what did it matter?

Attention Deficit

Thayer led the way. The ground was littered with cigarette butts and beer cans stripped by the rain. It was like visiting another planet. Clouds hung in the sky so thick they might've rained milk. I could see the moon, a hangnail sliver, although it was still daylight. I used to think it was following me, until Dad explained that it was always there, even when we couldn't see it.

"Where are we going?" I asked. "I mean, we should be getting back."

He grabbed my hand and pulled me along. "Who said we were going anywhere?"

"Oh. Okay."

We settled close to the edge of the canal. It wasn't far from school, but I'd never noticed it during my rides to class. This is how Florida used to look: a marsh lined with tall grass and windswept man-groves, their roots folded like hands.

"The water is so clear," Thayer said.

I turned and saw he was watching me.

When we reached the shore, I spotted a chain of pelicans on a rotten deck.

"Shh!" Thayer hissed. He held me back, his arm flung across my collarbone. "Be very quiet," he said in a low voice. Thayer reached into his jacket and pulled out a small metal pipe.

Thayer said, "Being bored alone is sad. But two people being bored is okay. It's going to rain again. Those telephone wires are going to give us cancer. Want to smoke?"

I stood in the shade and tried to look bored. "No thanks."

"You smoke trees?" he asked, and took a quick drag. Fumes spilled from his mouth.

"Yeah," I lied.

"I steal from my mom. She keeps her weed in a coffee can." He coughed so hard, it sounded like he was breathing through a straw.

"Doesn't it, like, mess with your asthma?"

"How do you know I have asthma?"

"Your inhaler."

"Yeah," he said. "But I usually use buckets, you know? Gravity bongs."

He jerked the pipe at me. I shook my head.

"You straight-edge or something?"

Most edgers didn't even "use" caffeine. They drew **X**'s on their hands and listened to hard-core bands like Black Flag. I almost wished I could relate to them, swear off aspirin, become a born-again vegetarian.

Out on the bay, a boater had run aground. He gunned his throttle and I thought about the manatees grazing in the shallow water.

"Weed should be legal," said Thayer. "I mean, have you ever met a violent pothead?"

"Uh, no."

"Smoking helps with my ADD. It keeps me from kicking the crap out of people who piss me off."

I thought about that day at school when he had beamed the tennis ball so hard, it broke the window. Then it made sense that Thayer was seeing a shrink. He had attention deficit disorder. ADD. Those three letters explained why he couldn't sit still in class.

The pipe crackled. Thayer said, "If everyone smoked weed, there would be more peace in this urban wasteland."

I laughed. Then I said something I immediately regretted.

"Did you take, like, medication? I mean, for your ADD?"

"I've been eating Ritalin since I was ten."

"Oh."

"But it makes me want to puke."

"I know," I told him.

He stared. "You on anything?"

My skin tingled. I couldn't think of how to sidestep his question, so I told the truth.

"I'm taking Paxil."

"Yeah?"

In the distance, the boater revved his engine. It's against the law to run a boat up on a flat, but that didn't stop them.

"Actually, I don't want to take it anymore."

Thayer nodded. "I would eat Ritalin like candy before I'd mess with Paxil again."

"You've tried it?"

"Sure. Paxil, Wellbutrin, BuSpar, Zoloft, Prozac," he said, tapping his fingers. This was enough to make my own fingers itch. I buried them in my pockets.

"Geez. Why so many?" I said.

"Because they don't work," he said. "At least, not for me."

Did they work for anybody?

"How long you been on it?" he asked.

"A few weeks."

"Even my mom's been on Paxil," he said. "Didn't do her any good."

Too many words. I couldn't concentrate. My own mother would be waiting in the school's empty parking lot, on a rampage if the nurse followed through with her phone call. I had to get out of there fast.

"Let's go back," I said.

Thayer flicked ash into the canal. "Ever see a

manatee?" he said, staring down into the water. "They're like dinosaurs. They move so slow, the boats just plow them over. People act like manatees don't belong in this city, like they're outcasts or something. But they've been here a long time, doing their own thing, you know? You've got to give them props."

"I've never seen one," I said. "Have you?"

Thayer slipped the pipe into his pocket. He slunk ahead, in some other time zone.

When we got to school, the streetlights were burning holes in my eyes. Maybe I had inhaled too much of Thayer's secondhand smoke. It was late, but the sky was blank, pure static.

Thayer stopped in front of the parking lot. Mama's rustbucket, a 1980s Nissan Stanza, flashed its headlights at us. I had to sneak away.

"That's my mom," I said. "I gotta go."

Thayer ambled toward the street. I could still see him, the way sparklers left marks in midair.

Seconds after he left, it started to drizzle. When I was trapped in the car, Mama asked about the "boy."

"I don't really know him," I said.

The windshield wipers squeaked. Mama put on the turn signal, pulled into the left lane, and let an ambulance pass. I spotted those flashing lights and imagined Mama in the hospital, pale walls in a pale room. I started counting traffic lights. One, two, three.

"Are you okay?" she asked, rubbing my head. "Do you want to tell me what happened at school today?"

No, I didn't.

"You used to be a straight-A student."

I watched the ambulance vanish into the rainstorm. Mama was driving too slow, white-knuckling the steering wheel.

Her tone dropped a notch. "Why are you behaving like this?"

"Like what?"

"Your voice is filled with anger all the time. You snap at me over nothing and then somehow it's my fault for feeling attacked," she said.

Of course my voice was filled with anger. I was angry at my parents for taking me away from my friends and then expecting me to behave like it was no big deal.

She pulled off at the exit. Although it never felt like autumn in Miami, cold-weather fashions crammed the store windows. Not that I could wear those fur "diva" coats or corduroy jackets. Not here.

Rain rolled off the dashboard, defying gravity. I picked at a hangnail.

"This isn't like you, Fin. I don't understand why you're acting out."

She stroked my hair. I had to be good, she said, and square things away.

"Just try a little harder," she said.

That was so much easier said than done.

Total Constant Order

"What would you like to talk about?" asked Dr. Calaban. She gestured toward the bookcase, crammed with her African violets.

I couldn't talk. It meant too much to her. I was holding back to maintain control over the situation, yet I never felt in control of anything.

"Okay," she said. "I'll go first."

She asked about my visit to the school nurse, but I didn't feel like spilling my guts. Now Dr. Calaban had other plans.

"I'd like to talk to your regular physician," she said, pronouncing the word like my French teacher, "fah-zeesh-yon." Dr. Calaban was a non-native like me. I wanted to ask if Haiti was dangerous, like they said on the news, all those murders and kidnappings. That's what a friend would've asked. But we weren't friends.

"One doctor is bad enough," I said.

She frowned. For a moment, I almost worried about hurting her feelings. "Let's get back to your routines."

"Who doesn't have routines?"

She watched my fingers.

"I can't stop counting," I admitted. "I even dream about numbers. Invisible armies of them."

Dr. Calaban wrote in her notebook.

"Frances, are you familiar with OCD?"

Did she say ADD? No, that was Thayer's problem.

"I think you might have obsessive-compulsive disorder." She peeled a Post-it note off her computer monitor, ripped a thin strip, and scribbled on it. I took the note and gawked at the words. The stickiness stayed on my fingers no matter how much I rubbed.

"Does that mean I'm losing my mind?" I asked.

Dr. Calaban folded her smooth brown hands.

"No, you're not losing your mind. OCD is also known as the doubting disease. This means that you often find yourself stuck on the same thoughts, spinning your wheels in circles." She made a loopy gesture, the bone bracelet clattering.

"So what are you going to do about it?"

"I'd like to up your prescription. Paxil has been known to help those with OCD. Should we give it a try?"

The last thing I needed was more Paxil. The side effects had grown so bad, they even leaked into my dreams at night. It was getting harder to tell the difference between my nightmares and my world when I was awake. Every morning, I found moon-shaped fingernail marks in my palms. My jaw ached from clenching my teeth. The pain seemed to last all day, although I never remembered when it began.

"Will the medicine make me feel any different?" I asked.

"Different in what way?"

I didn't answer.

"Are you talking about side effects? Because

Paxil can sometimes cause headaches."

I kept staring at her creepy skull bracelet.

"Frances, how is the Paxil making you feel?"

"Like crap," I told her.

"Okay," she said. "Can you give me more details?"

"There's no escape from it. Even my dreams are painful. I wake up with a stomachache, my head won't stop throbbing, everything tastes weird. I thought the meds were supposed to make me feel better, not worse."

Dr. Calaban looked surprised. "If you don't share what's going on, I can't help you. That is, if you want my help. What do you think? Can we work together?"

I thought for a second. "Yes," I said.

"Good. Then let's start by adjusting the dosage of your medication."

I groaned. "So I have to keep taking it?"

"For now," she said.

"How long is 'now'?"

"There are some people who choose to remain on antidepressants. But that's your decision. I would like you to continue taking it in conjunction with our sessions."

Who cared what she wanted? I had my own plans. That's when I decided to quit taking Paxil altogether. Not that she needed to know.

Her bracelet rattled as she scribbled in the notepad.

"What are you writing?"

"Should I share it with you?" she asked.

I nodded.

"Your obsessions are a means of gaining control. You couldn't stop your parents' divorce. I want you to see that you can take control in a more constructive way."

"How? Slitting my wrists?"

Her expression didn't change. "Are you being facetious?"

Dr. Calaban waited and didn't look away.

"Just kidding," I said. "I'm doing better, really. I'm not counting the clock so much anymore."

I stared at the potted violets. I wanted to slide my tongue across their whiskery leaves.

Dr. Calaban cleared her throat. "What do you

mean 'counting the clock'?"

"That's why I can't sleep."

"Frances," she said. "Why can't you sleep?"

I shifted in the chair, squeezing its legs like I'd done during our first session.

"I count while I do things."

"Like what?"

"Like brushing my teeth."

"Can you tell me what it feels like?" she asked. "Counting?"

"I can't stop doing it. If I lose count or finish on an odd number, then I have to start all over again."

Dr. Calaban locked her dark eyes on mine. I decided not to tell her the other part of my tooth-brushing obsession. I couldn't stop thinking about germs. A toothbrush is crawling with microscopic bugs. Amazing what you learn by watching the Discovery Channel.

"Do you know when you started counting?" she asked.

It was the last month of school before we left Vermont. I was lying in bed, unable to move.

When I think about my old room, I imagine it exactly the same, only dustier. There was a stuffed hound dog slumped by the door—its sole purpose, keeping my room open. Beside it was one of those cheesy lamps that glowed like a movie screen. (It depicted a forest fire, not the most comforting bedtime scene.)

A thought popped into my head. "I wish Dad would die." So I said the words out loud. "I wish Dad would die." The words just bubbled up. I tried to ignore them, but they kept rolling: "I wish Dad would die, I wish Dad would die." I tried thinking, "I love Dad," but it didn't help.

I glanced at the clock. If I could squash the words before the next minute rolled around, everything would be okay. I squeezed my arms against my chest and counted.

Eight minutes. Nine minutes. An uneven number. For some reason, it looked wrong, so I counted again. And again.

I couldn't go to class and concentrate on *A Tale of Two Cities* or the life cycle of a fruit fly or El Niño's effect on global weather patterns. I started counting everything in the room. I counted the boys with unlaced sneakers and the girls with curly hair. I counted stains on the ceiling and fingerprints in the window.

It was never enough.

N	O	V	E	M	B	E	R
14	15	22	5	13	2	5	18

Chester Copperpot

Thayer passed notes to me in class. Not the junior high variety, with felt-tip boxes along the margins: "Check 'yes' if you're bored." Thayer had other questions.

"If you could be happy for a year," he wrote, "but remember nothing, would you do it?

"Would you put up with horrible nightmares for the rest of your life if you could win a million dollars?

"Which is better: to die like a hero or in your sleep?"

I honestly didn't know.

For the entire week, Thayer would pass me a note before science class. His random thoughts took this order: electronic voting booths, the difference between Haitian voodoo and Cuban Santeria, night swimming, Internet blogs, and hairless cats. Soon I had a collection of notes hidden in my desk. I read them over and over until my eyes blurred.

At lunch, I sank back to earth. I knew that everyone was staring at Thayer and me. So we hid in the music room. Thayer materialized there with his binder and markers. He picked the lock with a paper clip and snuck into the empty room, with its thicket of music stands. We cranked the stereo, a dusty Panasonic that only played tapes. It was a relief dodging the lunchroom, with its sour popcorn smells and gossipy caste system.

Thayer wasn't born in the '80s, but he had memorized the decade in movie quotes.

"Come to me, son of Jor-el. Kneel before Zod."

"I'm a mog. Half man, half dog. I'm my own best friend."

"Chester Copperpot, Chester Copperpot."

"Sir, you are a vulgarian."

He could be Chunk in *The Goonies*, Barf in *Spaceballs*. Gasping, he ranted about Klingons and Kryptonite. He knew all the music: the stuttering beats of Kurtis Blow, the robotic bass lines of Big Daddy Kane.

His energy had an edge, as though he might combust, Wile E. Coyote–style, if I stopped paying attention. I was his audience, a human laugh track.

Thayer Pinsky could quote lines from commercials so ancient, they pre-dated the Internet.

"Crisp and clean and no caffeine."

"When you eat your Smarties, do you eat the red ones last? Do you suck them very slowly or crunch them very fast?"

Thayer said that it all started in elementary school. Fed up with his miserable grades, Thayer's mom dragged him to a doctor.

The doctor asked a lot of questions. "Do your thoughts bounce around like a pinball machine? Does your brain feel like a TV set with all the channels on?"

The night before a test, he found himself battling man-eating robots on the PlayStation or walking Bozo, his English bulldog. He wasn't lazy. When he studied between video game sessions, he felt okay. But when he sat at his desk, he couldn't concentrate.

The doctor offered Thayer a weapon.

Ritalin.

When Thayer swallowed the pill, he went to school and waited for the static to return when the meds wore off. Instead, he got a tingle between his eyebrows. In class, sitting quietly at his desk, he crunched up math equations like Pac-Man.

In the final hour of school, waiting for his second dose, his mood turned sour. Ritalin's magic didn't last long. At home, he took another pill. Soon he was tingling, though not like before.

He began to lose weight. His long, flat feet no longer fit his sneakers. He missed the way he used to feel, his needle hovering at ninety miles per hour. Most often, he floated in space.

"A group of foxes is called a 'skulk,'" Thayer said at lunch.

We were hiding in the music room, listening to gloomy old jazz records. It was getting late. Soon lunch would be over. Mr. Clemmons would shove his key in the lock any moment now.

"Sometimes they're also called a 'leash,'" he added.

Thayer reminded me of an orphaned animal.

His dad had split once Thayer started walking and talking. His mom worked in a hospital all the time, helping sick kids.

"She sees them more than me," he said. He was fiddling with his glove. If Thayer was in a bad mood, he wore a mechanic's glove on his left hand. He'd growl, "I'm agga-rah-vated." He'd been wearing that stupid glove for a week. Finally he took it off.

When I asked why, he said, "Because I'm not agga-rah-vated anymore."

Thayer couldn't've cared less about his SAT vocab. All day, he had doodled robots during class. Sometimes he'd write down his dreams. In them, he was always an animal—a lion, a dolphin, a fox. He believed that he morphed into these creatures.

"It's not the fact that my mom's dating," he told me. "It's the fact that she's replacing my dad. I don't need more adults in my life."

"My dad's dating someone. It's weird. But I guess it's good that my parents aren't together and fighting," I said.

"Yeah. I just wish Mom would wait until I was older."

I turned off the record. The melody spiraled out of measure. "Thayer, you're like one of the smartest people I know. Why are you bombing English?"

He shrugged. "Because it's tedious and I really don't care."

"You should care."

"Who gives a crap about mapping sentences? It bores me spitless. And poetry sucks beyond comprehension. My interpretation is always 'wrong' because it doesn't match the teacher's."

"But what about rap?" I asked. He was always writing rhymes on every available scrap of paper. "Isn't that poetry?"

That got his attention. "Look, I can handle writing on my own time. In class, it's different."

"True," I said.

"Besides . . . English is my last subject of the day. That's when my Ritalin wears off and I zone out."

I wanted to tell him about my Paxil nightmare. If anybody would understand how it messed with my head, it would be Thayer. But he had already switched gears.

"It doesn't help that I'm dyslexic," he said.

"Does that mean you see words backward?"

"No. That's what most people think." He jiggled his foot. "Really, it means I'm 'memory impaired.' Written words don't stick. So I bring a tape recorder to school."

A knot tightened my throat. I said, "Do you think you're, like, dependent on Ritalin to help you study?"

Thayer stared right into my eyes. Maybe he was examining his own reflection. "If you're trying to say I'm addicted, you're wrong."

"Don't get mad. I didn't mean to be in your face about it." I studied the clock on the wall. "We should get going."

He grunted. "Maybe I *am* hooked," he said. "Did you know that Ritalin belongs to the same class of drugs as cocaine? You can snort crushed Ritalin for a rush."

"Have you ever done it?"

He didn't answer.

"When I eat Ritalin, I'm not watching the clock, counting the seconds," he said.

Counting seconds was my forte.

123

"You don't know what it feels like," he added.

Yes, I did.

I chewed my lip. "Thayer, I want to tell you something."

"Yeah?" His foot hadn't stopped jiggling.

I yanked down the denim that had creeped up my thighs. There was no way to begin. I was ashamed of my "depression," a word that conjured Monday-morning blahs.

Thayer tapped my knee. "So what's crackin'?"

I was starting to get dizzy. "It's weird," I said. "You'll laugh."

Thayer tapped again, only this time, he didn't let go.

"I won't laugh," he said.

I believed him.

"Talk to me, Fin. We're buds, right?"

"Yeah. Sure," I said.

If that was true, then why was I staring at his hand—all five digits curled like they belonged on me? My own hand was trembling, getting ready to match Thayer's movement. That would mean evening out the gesture, in other words, skimming the hard shell of his kneecap.

So I did.

He didn't seem to mind.

There was the wheeze of a door unlocking. All the lights snapped on.

Mr. Clemmons hustled inside. Students were funneling into lines. Their voices droned.

"What are we going to do?" I whispered.

"We're gonna dip outta here," Thayer said.

Before I could stop him, Thayer snatched my hand, plowing a path through the maze of chairs and music stands. Kids stared. Mr. Clemmons was so flabbergasted, he only managed to croak, "Frances? What are you doing here?"

I could've strung him a paragraph of lies, but he wouldn't have heard it anyway. When we finally made it to class, Ms. Armstrong wrote our names on the board, a form of public humiliation.

I glanced at Thayer. He was too busy doodling to notice.

Tagging

'll show you how to drop a tag." Thayer ripped a page from his notebook and drew: *NERS*.

When I asked why he tagged the girls' bathroom, he said, "So you could see it."

I shoved him. "No, really. I want to know."

"I like it better in there," he said. "It smells nicer. Has a nicer view, too."

I sighed. No hope of getting a straight answer.

He scribbled graffiti the way I drew numbers, his hand squeezing the tip.

Thayer would tap my arm and say, "Check it." He would stare at a fence, at the block letters in thick black ink. Or a mailbox trimmed in balloon-shaped tags. He would explain how an Aerosol Prophet had tagged a Metro bus on Biscayne Boulevard.

"If you're gonna do a bus, then do it with style, man. Take it from me. When you go out to the street, hit it big."

And he talked about South Florida legends, the crews with names like INKHEADS, 7UP, BSK, DAM.

"This guy, Elite, has got some mad style. I caught a few fresh panels by him, some pretty dope murals. I personally don't like Krash's pieces letter-wise, but I give him props on bombing."

In time, I noticed. Everywhere I looked, there were codes in layers. If I spotted a tag, finger-traced on a dusty bumper, I was beaming.

An extravagant tag could send Thayer into such a dreamworld, he couldn't move until he had painted one of his own. He had tagged the school's metal bleachers near the football field. What he noticed, he wanted to copy. The bus tag, for example, could be better.

Thayer had seen me carving digits into desks. He asked me to show him my secret chain of numbers. So I snuck him into the girls' bathroom during lunch. We had to wait for Sharon Lubbitz and her clones to finish smearing their mascara. Then I opened the door and he strolled inside like he owned it.

"You've got some ill skills. Why did you do this?" he asked.

The question surprised me. "I don't know. It's just something I do. How did you get into it?"

"Nothing special. I started writing NERS a long time ago. Back then it seemed short, which is always good in the graf world, and it sounded like a cool name."

"Ever get caught?"

"Yeah, I was bombing in front of this store. Some security guards chased me around Sunset Place. I had to hide under a car until they rolled out. And I had red paint on my hands, like I had just murdered somebody."

Thayer reached into his jacket. He gave me his Sharpie pen. His fingers brushed mine and an electric jolt shot through them.

"You try," he said.

"I've never tagged here before. I just draw things."

"So what?"

"I'll get caught."

"No, you won't. I'll keep watch for you."

"I don't know."

"If you're going to be a smart bomber, you'll know what to hit and when to hit it."

He left me alone in the bathroom. I uncapped the Sharpie and sniffed ink. I scribbled NERS over the walls, across the mirrors, and down to the petal pink floor tiles. The untagged surfaces seemed too clean. I couldn't stop myself.

"Damn."

I didn't even notice that Thayer had returned. He stood back and studied my tags. He whistled. "That's tight."

For a while, we stood there, looking. Part of his unlaced Converse was bumping mine. Everything seemed out of the ordinary: His foot tapping my toe. The mere concept of toes.

I knew from his expression that I had done well. More than well. My tags looked solid, the edges outlined in thick halos. Already, I felt the urge to tag again.

"Yo, we gotta dip," he said.

By the end of the day, the school was buzzing about the graffiti in the girls' bathroom. Everyone believed that a boy had trespassed into that forbidden zone and left his filthy mark. The teachers questioned Thayer. His notebooks were infested with ballpoint NERS tags, just like those on the pastel tiles. Since nobody would come clean, the principal made Thayer scrub the stains with nail polish remover.

The NERS incident didn't do much for Thayer's popularity. But the four-letter stares and acid-laced insults rolled off him. He didn't even pay attention.

On Saturday, we walked from our houses to the Metrorail station near the park, which dumped its passengers in a nowhere zone of treeless sidewalks. He brought his skateboard and I pretended I knew how to ride it. We went to the mall, where Thayer made up voices for the pigeons. Around him, I didn't count so much anymore. Tagging kept my head and hands working in total constant order.

Just watching Thayer wind his streaky hair into a knot was a landmark moment—the same when he recited the alphabet in Spanish or when he ate a bowl of Cocoa Puffs for lunch, sipping the last drop of tinted milk. I liked the sight of him marching into our hideout, the music room, his banged-up skateboard at his side like a faithful steed. He'd wrestle it up the stairs and lean it against the wall. I couldn't help wondering why he felt comfortable doing these things in front of me.

On the way home on Saturday, we were writing tags on each other's hands.

"So what was your first impression of me?" he asked.

I didn't know what to say. I thought about him sitting alone on the bench that day at lunch and throwing the tennis ball so hard, it broke the window.

"You seemed kind of angry," I said.

"Huh," he said. "It sucks that you saw me that way. Sometimes I get pissed when my Ritalin wears off."

I was counting the syllables in his sentences. He spoke super fast, in 8/8 time, while most people talked in plain old 4/4 rhythm.

"So your emotions are, like, all over the place," I said.

"Yeah," he said. For once, he was quiet.

"Hey," I said. "So what did you think of me?"

He perked up again. "I thought you were a rock star."

"Liar," I said.

"Why would I lie?" he asked, genuinely confused.

"So what makes me a rock star? I can hardly play the violin."

"But you have perfect rhythm. And you always wear that '80s jacket. So hard-core. Nobody in the entire school looks like you."

"That's sad." I covered my face in my hands.

"No. It's good." Thayer pulled my hands away. "Quit hiding." He wrote a row of numbers on the inside of my wrist. "Now write yours," he said. "Just in case."

"Just in case what?" I asked, staring at those inky digits, half expecting them to float away.

"In case I need to talk to a rock star," he said.

I scribbled my number on his skin.

A Perfect Day for the Answering Machine

jumped every time the phone rang. And then, one weekend, Dad called.

He came to the house and picked me up as if we were on a date. It had been raining nonstop all afternoon. Mama didn't say much besides, "Hello, David" and "Drive carefully." Then I noticed Yara in the passenger seat of his brand-new BMW.

The restaurant, La Carreta, was a chain on Eighth Street with sugarcane sprouting all over the lawn. Dad took control of the menu so I'd know how sophisticated he had become since dating his girlfriend. She was wearing a low-cut sweater, the fuzzy kind that sheds like a cat. Mohair, I think it's called. Yara's big hair almost disguised the fact that she was closer to my age than Dad's.

"I'm so excited to meet you, Frances," she gushed. "Your father talks about you all the time."

I didn't want to know anything about this woman.

The coffee arrived and Yara sipped it. She tossed her hair and asked, "Don't you want a taste?" The café con leche smelled good. At home, Mama never let me drink coffee because she thought it would stunt my growth.

I noticed a lipstick stain on the rim and pushed the mug away.

Dad beamed at us. He was dressed like a tourist—wraparound sunglasses and a pleated guayabera with the top buttons undone. I figured he had called to talk about Christmas vacation, but actually, he wanted me to meet his new girlfriend. I felt abandoned. Or worse: replaced by Yara.

"A toast," Dad said. "To the ladies at my table: May the most you wish for be the least you get." This was something he always said at family functions.

We clinked our mugs. Dad slung his arm around

Yara and turned toward me. "So, grasshopper. How's school?"

This is what Dad did best, torture me about my failures.

"It's okay, I guess."

At the mention of school, Yara perked up. "I still remember the dress I wore to my first boy-girl dance. I was a little upset that another girl wore the same thing, but everyone said I looked great in it."

Of course she remembered. It wasn't that long ago.

"You're going to have so much fun. This is the time you'll remember forever," she said.

Anyone who uses those ad slogans is lying.

I nibbled a plantain chip. I thought about somebody's dirty hands tossing them on my plate and my stomach flip-flopped. I was starving, yet I couldn't eat anything. I tried to count my nausea away. The menu made no sense: Oxtail stew. Pigs' Feet Andalusian. Midnite Sandwich. Tamale wrapped in a corn husk. Yuca fries. FuFu mashed potatoes.

Yara talked about who she hung out with in

ninth grade and who she dated and I don't know what else.

Counting wasn't working at that moment, so I slipped a hand in my pocket, stroking the tweezers that I had stolen from Mama. I pushed on the sharp edges. One, two, three times. It hurt so bad, I winced.

Yara asked, "Are you seeing anyone special?"

My pulse thumped. "Not really."

Yara tapped Dad's arm. "I bet she has a secret boyfriend."

"I hope not," he said, drumming the table in 8/8 time.

"Are you sure?" Yara said.

"I'm sure I don't have a boyfriend."

"You're kidding. A pretty girl like yourself should be out there, exploring life."

Dad scraped back his chair. "You're mature for your age. I don't imagine many boys have the nerve to approach you."

Dad didn't ask about my love life. He never did. Instead he pestered me about school. What did I plan to do in the "real world"?

I pressed harder. The pain spread up my hand.

"I want to paint," I said.

For a moment, nobody spoke. Then our food arrived. Dad grabbed a fry off my plate. I couldn't stand it when Dad picked at my food without asking. He said, "You know, I went to school for music. That was a mistake."

I'd heard all this before.

Back in our real house, Dad spent a lot of time hiding in the basement, which he called "the hovel." He stored his telescope there, along with his college stuff, a shrine to the 1970s. The walls were painted jet black and perfectly matched the velvet paintings of tigers and astrology signs that he tacked all over the place. I used to stroke them with one finger, as if the big cats could actually purr.

Dad let me thumb through his psychedelic record collection, stacked to the ceiling in milk crates. We played them on his hi-fi. The FM stations were "on the fritz" but I'd sink back in Dad's beanbag chair, clutching his Gandalf pillow, and listen to those lipsticked men locked inside the albums, wailing about soul survivors and spiders from Mars.

Best of all, Dad let me sit on his knee while he pounded on his drum set.

"You're damaging her ears," Mama said.

Not that it stopped him from teaching me the flamadiddle and open roll. With my fists gripping the sticks, his hands cupped over mine, we played along to his records. Of course, I thought it was me drumming instead of Dad.

A cork lamp with a fuzzy shade flickered near his drum set, stapled with the buttons he used to pin on his suspenders during his bartending days: "Kiss me! I'm Irish!" or "Smiling is an early warning sign of a stroke." Dad pinned those buttons on my T-shirts. He stapled a moonish face to my collar. The button's mouth stretched like an arrow. "Have a day," the caption read.

I came home from school one afternoon and discovered that Mama had sold all the buttons in a box, along with a few of my plastic Breyer horses, at her annual tag sale. I didn't speak to her for a week. I would communicate through Dad and say things like, "Tell *her* I left my book bag in the car."

I wanted to ask Dad if he remembered any of

this, but he was too busy cuddling up to Yara. I stared out the window, past my half-eaten chicken mojo, watching what Thayer called the "moving sidewalk" of waterlogged people. A man with a shaved head drifted past, trying to shield himself with a newspaper. He reminded me of a Hare Krishna who Thayer and I had seen in a coffee shop one day after school.

"But you hate coffee," I had told Thayer. Why would the philosopher who doesn't drink coffee take me out for coffee?

"Yeah, it's very Zen of me," he had said, slumped on the edge of the chair, swinging his long legs in circles. "Or we could play bingo," he continued, on a roll. "Or try the dog track. Which do you prefer?"

"All of the above."

Thayer said he'd write a song about me. Then he kissed my nose.

Nobody had ever smooched my nose before. I was so frazzled, I couldn't look at him. So I stood in the doorway of the café and closed my eyes. And he kissed them, too.

I didn't know what to make of these kisses. So what if he'd smooched every inch of my face except my mouth? In Miami, nobody shook hands. They pecked your left cheek—an invasion of personal space that made everyone seem far friendlier than they were in reality.

I thought about how I'd react if his lips landed on the lower hemisphere of my face. At first I had avoided him, like Sharon and the other girls at school. But who was I to judge Thayer? I hadn't risen to the top of the social totem pole. Kissing him couldn't ruin my nonexistent reputation. That is, if he kissed me back.

These thoughts had never entered my head until recently. We were walking to the canal after drinking our coffees and the sun was splintering between the mangroves. I was rattling on about my Siamese fighting fish, a stubby-tailed female I had named Stella after an Interpol song. Thayer was listening so hard, I lost my concentration. He listened as if I were the most interesting person on the planet. I was looking at the sunlight in his eyes, and then I knew what I couldn't admit before.

Any girl would be lucky to kiss him.

So what did he expect me to do? He was always laughing. Half the time, I couldn't figure out why.

Maybe he was laughing at me.

"Chica, you're bleeding," Yara said. She was staring at the blood-spattered napkin.

I tried to wipe it off. The tweezers clattered on the floor.

Yara reached under the table. "Is this yours?"

"Thanks."

Dad snatched my hand. "What did you do here?"

My throat clenched. Suddenly I was walking past two, three, four tables and I don't know how many staring customers.

In the ladies' room, a ponytailed girl was taking her time, washing at the sink. I tucked my hands behind my back, but she saw anyway. From the look on her face, I guess I must have scared her.

I had been thinking about Thayer. He had disappeared after that walk. Vanished. Bailed on me. On Friday, I waited in the music room, but he didn't show up. I sat there like a loser until the bell rang. I imagined him making fun of me with his cooler-than-thou skater comrades. His nose kiss was a joke. I was the punch line.

The door banged open. It was Yara.

"Need some help?"

I pumped the soap dispenser, but it was empty.

"No paper towels, either," she said. "But we can wing it."

She smothered my cut in toilet paper. Before I could think about germs, she squeezed her fingers around mine, gripping so hard I could feel her pulse.

I stood there, looking at the bandage.

The little girl left without bothering to dry her hands. Now Yara and I were alone.

"You can talk to me, chica," Yara said. "I'm a good listener."

I sank against the wall, melting like the witch in *The Wizard of Oz*, dribbling into the ground, down under the restaurant.

"Come on," she said.

"Give me a minute."

Yara frowned. I could tell she didn't want to leave me alone. When she finally left the bathroom, I could still smell her perfume. I felt Mama's tweezers in my pocket.

I took them out and yanked at my eyebrows, first the left, then the right, until my arches were pencil-straight. When I tugged, the hairs pulled out easily. Their roots were pale white, each with a little nub.

"What took you so long?" Dad asked when I returned to the table. He touched my forehead. It stung. "Your face looks a little flushed. You're not catching that bug that's been going around, are you?"

Yara was watching me.

"I'm fine," I said.

We were getting ready to leave the restaurant, and Dad was gathering his raincoat and laughing at some joke I hadn't caught. It seemed like everyone else in the restaurant had heard it, because they were all laughing, even the girl in the flower print dress on the porch.

Dad hugged me so hard, I lifted off the ground.

Yara smooched me on the cheek and said, "Have fun, chica. You're supposed to be having fun." Her kiss print burned my skin. She laughed. So did Dad. We were laughing because we didn't know what to say.

Round Numbers

The number ten was a round drum with a thin stick. Ten minutes into a test left me looking for numbers, as if counting could snap off the lights or fire up the pencil sharpener (not to mention the air-conditioning). How could I concentrate when I was dying in slow motion? One minute my teeth knocked together, as if I had morphed into an ice sculpture. The next minute, sweat dribbled down my back and I could smell everyone breathing on me, the air so warm and soupy.

Taking Paxil was like having the rug pulled out from under my brain cells. So I quit. I didn't plan on popping pills for the rest of my life. I wanted to declare myself "cured" and go on without the neuro-chemical cocktail. I couldn't tell Dr. Calaban because I was afraid she would prescribe more medication.

Dr. Calaban wanted me to be happy artificially. If that didn't work, she'd toss me in the loony bin and turn me into an ever-smiling idiot.

Quitting made me feel sicker.

Paxil's aftereffects had turned my body into a busted thermostat. I had sworn off the drug and it still hadn't left my system. I was contaminated.

I glued my eyes to the door and prayed that I wouldn't throw up.

At school, the windows were bolted with metal bars "for our safety." I was thinking how those so-called security bars could trap us during a fire when the alarm buzzed. Ms. Armstrong didn't even look up from her desk. I wished that she'd take off her stupid hat. Mama said it was bad luck wearing hats indoors.

"Second false alarm this week. Somebody thinks they're funny," Ms. Armstrong said, popping a grape in her mouth. Lately, she'd been eating during class, which didn't seem fair. For example, she'd pull a wrinkly avocado out of her purse, as if it had grown there, and gobble the whole thing with a spoon. The last thing I needed to see was Ms. Armstrong chewing.

"What if it's the real deal?" Thayer blurted. He never raised his hand. "We'd be torched like KFC. Then my mom would sue the school."

Ms. Armstrong said, "Quiet, please," which seemed pointless, given that a fire alarm was buzzing in the background. As she wove between the desks, she asked, "Did anyone lose power during last night's storm?"

Thayer's hand shot up. It was just him and this weird girl from England. Two hands.

Brit-girl wrinkled her nose. "It's absolutely disgusting," she said in this bitchy voice, reminding me of Posh Spice or the unfunny comedies on PBS. "You can't even flush the toilet without running water."

The boys in the back row, all burnouts, laughed and made flushing sounds with their mouths. Ms. Armstrong told them to shut up (or "restrain themselves"). Thayer rambled on about the evils of Florida Power and Light and how they should bury the power lines underground.

The lava in my stomach had morphed into needles. I squirmed in my chair, trying to find a position that didn't prick me.

Don't throw up. Don't throw up. Don't throw up.

Thayer passed me a note folded like a ninja star. Once he got rolling, forget it. He'd never finish that test. He was too busy writing about his latest conspiracy theory: HAARP, a tuning fork in the ocean, was steering hurricanes toward Miami.

"This is just practice," he scribbled. "Biological warfare is only the beginning. Weather weapons can wipe out an entire nation in a matter of hours."

Last week he was obsessed with bird flu, "which is, like, five species away from hurting humans. Just propaganda to get people to buy vaccines."

I sat in my hard plastic chair, ripping my test and thinking about the number five. I was so busy juggling it around in my head, I didn't even notice Ms. Armstrong staring at me. The entire class turned around and my throat itched.

"I don't feel good. Can I go to the restroom?" I asked. My throat wouldn't stop itching.

I needed to rinse my mouth.

She shook her head no. The fumes from her dry erase marker tickled my nostrils. I felt my brain cells dying. I swear it.

Thayer tapped my shoulder. I ignored him. He kept tapping one, two, three more times and I scooted my desk an inch away from him. He was talking about tuna fish . . . or how he lived off it, even though it's "crawling with mercury."

My stomach gurgled. I couldn't focus on my test. I stared at all those blank spaces reserved for "short answers" and saw a stack of minus signs.

"I'm not sure what to write," said Thayer, erasing craters into his paper.

Ms. Armstrong got up and glanced over Thayer's shoulder. He had written everything Ms. Armstrong had scribbled on the blackboard, including the instructions ("back up your answers with examples").

"Now give me your own ideas," said Ms. Armstrong, squinting under her hat.

Teachers always said stuff like that. What they really meant was: Memorize my ideas, but make them sound like your own.

The fire alarm wouldn't quit. I scribbled triangles across my test, trying to cancel out the buzzer. Somebody bumped my desk. I craned down at Thayer's slip-on Converse, which were dappled with doodles, a pirate skull and crossbones. Sweet. I could've decorated my own snow white sneakers, but I didn't have the guts.

I tapped his toe with my pencil. One, two, three.

Thayer coughed so hard, he drowned out the alarm. Whenever he started hacking like that, a knot tightened in my chest. He sounded sicker than me.

"You sure this isn't for real?" he called between coughs. "I smell smoke."

I glanced at Thayer's paper again. Amazing. We'd been sitting for a half hour and he hadn't jotted two paragraphs.

I put down my pencil.

Just then, the principal barged into the classroom. He leaned in the doorway, letting in noise and sunlight. Everyone stopped pretending to take the test and stared. So did Ms. Armstrong, who had moved on to her moldy-looking avocado. I'd seen the principal only at assemblies, lurking behind a podium, so I wasn't sure if he had legs. Maybe he wasn't sure either, due to the size of his waist.

"Why aren't you moving?" he said, mopping his neck with a hanky. "This isn't a false alarm, people."

A few girls screamed. Others kept working on the test.

Thayer rocketed out of his chair and said, "I knew it!"

"Single file," said Ms. Armstrong, despite the mob clogging our exit.

I didn't budge. No use getting trampled.

Ms. Armstrong yanked me into the aisle. "Now," she said.

I stumbled and hit the floor. Once I was down in the forest of desk legs, I just stretched out on the carpet.

"Up," she said. So much for sympathy.

I looked up. There was a secret world under our desks: stalactites of gum and Scotch tape, metal staples gleaming. You could get lost in it—clues in the empty classroom like archaeological evidence.

And then I saw it: the tennis ball wedged under a cabinet, all fluffy with dust.

Ms. Armstrong flung out a hand. I ignored it and finally scrambled to my feet. Once outside, we joined the rest of the class, which had spilled around the flagpole in the parking lot.

As we stood outside, I caught a hint of something charred in the breeze. The fire alarm clanged and the jocks snickered.

"Smells like burned tortillas," said Sharon.

"The smoke alarm went off. Was someone smoking?" the principal muttered. He stood there, looking confused, as the girls mulled around, screaming and laughing.

The sun hit my face. So did the moist green smell of mowed grass. I chewed my lip and counted to three, praying I wouldn't puke.

It didn't work.

I doubled over and retched dry air. Amazing. Even when I tossed my cookies in front of the entire school, it was a nonevent.

A hand grabbed my left shoulder. I touched the other side to make it even. Thayer stood there, talking loud. "Hey, shortie," he said. "You feeling okay?"

Lava climbed up my throat and leaked into my mouth. I aimed for the grass, missed, and spat chunky goo onto the sidewalk.

"Oh my God. That's so gross," said Sharon. "Maybe she's preggers. Oh, wait. That's impossible."

Sharon and her crew were comparing muscles with a couple jocks in Straight Edge hats. Seconds ago, they had been bragging about getting wasted. These kids reminded me of zombies, grinning wide, even though the school could go down in flames. Or not. After all, it was built entirely of concrete.

I glanced at faces I didn't recognize, their glazed expressions, and wondered who was taking medication. I knew nothing about these kids, despite spending six hours a day with them, week after week. I knew more by looking under their desks.

"Yo, shortie," said Thayer, edging closer. "I got some good shit. This will fix what's illing you. Let me hook it up." He jiggled the pipe on his key chain, right there, in front of everyone. Ms. Armstrong didn't notice. She was too busy trying to keep everyone in single file. If she saw the pipe, she'd probably mistake it for a tire gauge or something.

He pushed it into my hand. The pipe was shaped like a metal mushroom, which kind of gave it away.

"I can't handle this right now," I said, passing it back.

Thayer shrugged. "I'm just spitting out some knowledge for you."

"So where were you at lunch the other day?" I asked.

He didn't answer. Thayer was an expert changer of subjects. "Hey, your hair is getting longer." He smoothed a few strands off my forehead.

"I'm growing it out," I said, although I hadn't thought about it before.

"It looks dope," he said.

"Thanks," I said as a sunburn crawled up my neck. "Actually, it's getting on my nerves. I need to tie it back or something."

"You want to borrow this?" Thayer whipped off his bandanna and slid it over my head. "I got it from the army surplus store in Homestead." He tightened the knots until it fit just right. I felt lighter with my hair pushed back, not to mention a little tougher.

"It smells like you," I said. God, that was dumb.

He grinned. "Don't you love it when somebody borrows your junk and brings it back and it smells exactly like their house? That's, like, the best."

"True." I was gulping deep breaths. The air was so full.

"You ever grow it really, really long? Like down to your butt?" he asked.

"No," I said, trying to imagine how that would look. "My mom wouldn't let me. She said it tangled too easily. So it's time I took control of my hair."

"You should've seen my locks in the beginning," he said. "My boy Marco and me . . . we twisted them with honey. Then they just rotted and fell out."

"Yuck," I said. "What do you use now?"

"Wax. Or cactus juice," he said.

Before I could ask where he found that stuff, he took out his Sharpie and started painting my split ends. "When it gets longer, we can dye the tips black."

"Cool," I said, wondering how Mama would react to butt-length black hair.

Thayer got bored with his dried-out marker and tossed it in the street. "We've been standing here for nine minutes and twenty-eight seconds," he said, glancing at his calculator watch.

My brain juggled a trio of threes, then added two and eight into ten. We gazed up at the power lines, which were decorated with countless sneakers, all mangled and dangling like tongues.

"When a gang member dies, they toss their victim's shoes up there," said Thayer.

I didn't know whether to believe him.

He took out the tiniest Ziploc bag I'd ever seen—about the size of a postage stamp—and sprinkled its leafy contents into his pipe.

"Sure you don't want to hit it?" he asked.

My tongue still tasted molten. What difference did it make? I'd already had one drug pumping through my bloodstream and it hadn't done much good.

"You're going to smoke right now?" I asked.

"Yep." He was already messing with the lighter.

"In front of everyone?" I said.

"Who's gonna care?" he asked.

I glanced at the mob of teachers and students standing there, waiting for something to happen. Nobody was paying attention to us. They never did.

"Okay," I said.

"Follow me," he said, all serious.

We stepped out of the line and moved toward the seniors, who were sucking water from the fountains and spitting it at one another. That's when I looked up at the second floor, where the upperclassmen prowled the breezeway, and noticed the flames. Somebody's locker was on fire.

"Told you I smelled smoke," said Thayer. "The seniors burn the shit out of their lockers whenever there's a major test. It's practically a tradition."

The fire seemed brighter than everything else. The rest of the school was black and white. I watched the gnat-sized bits of paper billow in the smoke.

"Just a little excitement," said the principal,

pushing us in line with the cackling seniors, although we didn't belong there. The flames wiggled back and forth, making no sound.

Thayer coughed and covered his face. He was looking at the truck parked across the street: Metro Dade Fire Rescue.

"I've been in one of those," he said, not bothering to explain.

"Ya'll need to get back," yelled a sweaty fireman, materializing from thin air. He looked like an astronaut in a suit that could withstand nuclear clouds. I imagined him playing with fire trucks as a kid.

"You going to put that out or not?" the principal asked.

"I'll take care of it, sir," said the fireman, who probably posed for nonprofit calendars. He still wasn't doing anything.

By this time, most of the classes had meandered around the flagpole. They gawked at a safe distance while the principal had a long discussion with the fireman.

"Hey." Thayer nudged me. He was pinching this stubby pipe between his fingers. After flaming

up and taking a few gut-busting puffs, he pa
to me.

I'd heard the "Just Say No" spiel since fifth
grade. By now, it seemed like a joke.

"Put your finger over the hole while you hit it.
Let go before you finish inhaling," he said. This was
the boy who was sent home from school, all for
wearing a shirt that said D.A.R.E. in bold red letters.
Beneath it were the words "Drugs Are Really
Expensive."

I took a deep breath, as if diving underwater. I
had never smoked a cigarette before, much less
pot. I tried to imitate the way Thayer took these
tiny sips of smoke, but, of course, I coughed like
a first timer.

"Hold it in," he said.

That was the last thing I wanted to do. I pictured
the human lungs in my biology book: twin willows
with cascading branches. Now they burned like the
rest of me, the flames twirling up my throat.

It didn't taste like anything I'd sniffed at con-
certs, that wet carpet stench that fogged up the air.
So far, I wasn't blasting off or craving nachos or

...arking lot. I felt like a complete

...crew were a few feet away,
...would've crawled off and hid.
...y voice coming out strange,

"...ey, Fin," said Sharon. "I hear you don't
like me."

I turned around. "Yeah, that's right. What are
you going to do about it?"

Sharon tried to giggle, but nobody joined in. It
was just her, alone.

"Those girls are dogs with a capital *B*," said
Thayer.

I laughed even harder.

Thayer stared at me. "Don't Bogart that weed,"
he said, snatching back the pipe.

A grungy sophomore (whose name I had forgotten) shuffled toward Thayer. He was the boy with
the skully cap I'd seen at the park, but he looked so
much older than us. Tufts of hair sprouted on his
knuckles and knees, even between his eyes.
Stretched over his gut was this lame Hawaiian shirt

(no doubt for "ironic" effect). At first, I thought he might call us out. My panic surged into words.

"Hey, what's up?" I said, looking at my shadow, which had merged with his.

He grabbed the pipe from Thayer without even asking.

"Yo, T-Puff," the kid said. His voice was low and startling. "You used to get me some awesome chronic. Now you're dropping it on this chicken-head?"

"I got nada, bro," said Thayer. "You out thievin' again?"

"Whatever, tool." He turned and looked at me as if I had dropped out of the sky. "We met before?"

"I don't think so," I said, watching the grass, which seemed to be swelling.

He snorted. "Must've been one of Thayer's other girlfriends."

I glanced at Thayer, who looked away. He flicked the guy's head and they both started chattering in Spanish, which reminded me of ribbons curling. I can't stand it when people *habla Español* in front of me, as if I didn't exist. I always think that they're saying something rude. In this case, it was probably true.

"You speak Spanish?" I asked Thayer.

He took a deep bow and said, "*Sí, chica*. My grandma? In New York, remember? She's from Cuba. But her blood goes back to Galicia, this part of Spain that was taken over by the Celts, which is why we've got light eyes and—"

"What's up with that freaky sweater?" said Mr. Oh-So-Cool Sophomore, blowing smoke straight up in the air.

I wasn't sure whether he was talking to me or about me. "I'm cold, you know?"

"Cold?"

"In class, right? Because they turn the air-conditioning up so high," I answered.

"You mean 'low,'" Thayer added.

"Then you go outside and it's like a hundred degrees. I'm roasting to death because I haven't figured out how to dress for this climate."

Mr. Oh-So-Cool Sophomore took another hit, then passed the pipe to Thayer. "You going skiing in the Alps or something?" he said.

"You should talk," I said, "with that knit cap on your head."

Where had that come from?

He kept talking to Thayer as if I were invisible. Their conversation consisted of mumbles and grunts, along with outdated wigger slang and the occasional four-letter word. I stood back and watched the smoke signals pouring from the open locker. Alone with Thayer, I could talk about sea-horses and secret dimensions. We had developed our own code words, like "gravy train," for Sharon's doglike worshipers. And when some desperate girl tried to break into their clique, we'd say that she had "fallen into a trance," because she couldn't think on her own. Now he was acting trancelike around this brain-dead poseur who was just one grade ahead of us. We weren't speaking the same language anymore.

Maybe it was the weed electrifying my nerves or the constant jolt from my chemical headache. I couldn't stand there, watching the trees flicker, being invisible, being "that girl."

I got back in line with the rest of our class, which

had begun to file toward my homeroom.

"Fin, wait," Thayer said, moving toward me and stumbling on nothing. That boy was such a klutz.

I kept walking. I couldn't help wondering how often Thayer got high and how I would handle going back to class stoned. Since I didn't talk much, I doubted anybody would notice. With twenty-three in our class, Ms. Armstrong was always distracted with louder, more attention-needy losers than me.

At the count of ten, I turned to see if Thayer was still behind me. He wasn't. Maybe he had gone to the canal to smoke with the manatees. All the stoners knew about that spot, though in the beginning, I'd believed it was our secret. I was just catching on to a lot of stuff. That was the difference between us.

Something rustled behind a car, catching my attention. Crouching down, I spied rows of plasticky legs rising in slow motion. Land crabs. The grass was swarming with them. I watched them, fascinated by their mechanical movements. If Thayer had stuck around, he might've given them names, as well as voices. He could be so many things.

Days later, I'd stumble over broken limbs—bits of crab pinchers that might crack open a beer. Then came the heat. Then the stink. Then I'd find only their holes—empty, abandoned, like a question waiting to be answered.

Split Ends

When Mama wasn't giving me the silent treatment, just like she did with Dad, we were fighting over my emotions, which, apparently, she knew more about than me.

It started during another of Mama's cleaning fits. Mama always got a major thrill when she dumped out her purse. This was her religion. She shoved her keys and coins in plastic bags, the same kind in which Thayer carried his weed. She kept her credit cards in an old eyeglass holder, her loose change in a sock. Standing in the checkout line at Publix, I wanted to kick down the candy racks like dominoes after watching her whip that ratty thing at the cashier and pay completely in change.

When she spilled pennies all over the floor, I

kept finding them everywhere, wedged in the carpet. I'd step on one and it would stick to my heel. I hated pennies, all those single digits rolling on forever.

Just touching a gunked-up green penny made my skin crawl. I collected as many as I could find and threw them in the trash, making sure not to touch the rim. Then I scrubbed my hands with antibacterial soap. As I stood at the kitchen sink, pumping the dispenser (shaped, for some reason, like an aquarium), Mama said I'd made a mess.

"I just bleached that out. Now you're wasting water and it's dirty again," she said, wiping the faucet with a paper towel. Talk about wasteful. Ten thousand trees were chopped down just because she refused to use a sponge, which, according to Mama, swarmed with bacteria.

"Big deal," I said. "Sinks are supposed to be used, not looked at."

Mama wadded up the paper towel and pitched it into the garbage bag. Not a trashcan like normal families keep in the kitchen. Mama preferred the brown paper bags we got from the grocery store.

"It's cleaner that way," she said.

They filled so fast, they overflowed. How clean was that? On top of everything else, the bags were decorated with geometric snowflakes, not that it ever snowed in Miami.

"Something's leaking on the floor," I said, taking a step backward.

"Oh, shoot," said Mama, who never swore. Ever. She plunked the entire bag inside a Hefty Cinch Sack. "Would you like to take this outside?" she asked, dragging it toward me.

"Not really," I said.

"Can you help me out?" she asked.

I could. But why should I?

That's when she heard the jingling.

"Fin, what did you put in here?" she asked.

"Nothing," I said, scrubbing faster.

Of course, she had to peek inside. She must've spotted all those pennies rolling around with our banana peels and empty tuna cans.

"You threw away money," she said, her voice rising. "Why would you do such a thing?"

I stood with my hands dripping. "I don't know."

"Now you're getting the floor wet," she said, ripping off another super-absorbent paper towel and shoving it at me. Down went another tree.

"They're just pennies," I said. "It's not like you can buy anything with one cent. The government should stop making them."

"Pennies add up to dollars," she said, as if I hadn't passed kindergarten. An image flashed in my head: a hundred pennies sparkling in the fountain at the Boston Common park.

"I want you to take out those pennies," said Mama. "Now."

I tried to explain but you couldn't tell her anything. "There's no reason for you to be yelling at me right now. And I'm not putting my hands in there," I said.

Mama gripped my arm in a death lock and tugged me toward the trash. She shoved my hand in deep. I rooted around the damp and gritty coffee grounds until I pulled out a penny.

"There. Are you satisfied?" I said, flinging it at her.

"I want all of them, Frances," she said.

"Do it yourself," I said. By this time, I was

169

sobbing. "I hate living with you. Why can't I be with Dad?"

Mama raised a finger to her lips as if she had said it instead of me. "I don't know you anymore," she said. "You push me away. And the less I know, the more worried I am."

"Well, you haven't a clue what's going on with me," I said. My stomach was a lava pit. My head was an electrical storm.

How could she know what was going on? She spent the entire day talking to strangers, then dragged herself on the couch and plopped in front of the television. At night, she creeped around the house and stayed up until the newspaper zinged across the lawn. I would hear the TV's telltale hum, even with the volume muted. (Mama clicked across the dial without sound.) Once, I stuffed the remote under a sofa cushion. I watched Mama hunt for it. After a while, she propped her feet against the TV and changed channels with her toes.

"Why are you so angry all the time?" she asked.

I laughed. "I'm not."

She threw up her hands. "Okay. You know everything."

If I wasn't angry before, I was now. "Why are you telling me this?"

"I don't want to discuss it," she said.

So I didn't tell her anything. I marched into my room and slammed the door. Behind it, I heard "smooth jazz" burbling from the so-called entertainment center in the living room—goosey saxophones and violins. How could she find that stuff relaxing? Listening to it made me want to stab myself. Repeatedly.

I grabbed my headphones, sat in the plastic chair by my desk, and cranked the volume. My outdated mix tapes pushed me back to a place I really couldn't handle anymore. The tape wasn't helping so I clicked over to FM. Nothing but reggaeton and people rapping in Spanglish. Radio in South Florida just plain sucked. At least the stations in Burlington played music, most of the time.

I missed my old life in Vermont so badly, even my body had fallen out of sync. For example, my period, which never checked in like clockwork, had gone completely schizoid. Each month it grew lighter until it finally disappeared. But who cared? It wasn't like I had a reason to worry. Except for one thing: When it was AWOL, I battled the worst case of cramps, doubling over as an invisible rake scraped my guts.

Maybe I needed to put on a few more pounds. When I started taking Paxil, my appetite went out the window. I just couldn't keep anything down. The plastic chair dug into my bones, making me shift and fidget. No matter how I moved, I couldn't find a comfortable spot.

Moving to my bed, I thought about tweezing every blond hair on my big toe. Instead, I reread a note that Thayer had stuffed in my backpack:

"I am practicing looking up while I write this so that it will fool Ms. Armstrong. It has worked so far! She's so dumb she's falling for it. Notice how my handwriting changed? That's because I was writing on my book. But now I'm writing on my desk. Did you know that the Food Network is filmed like porn? Well, gotta go. Wow. I bet you feel good knowing all this stuff (just joking). Well, I have nothing else to say. I might even write again someday."

This was proof: That kid was crazy.

When I finally got sick of sitting around, I left my room and heard Mama talking sickly sweet to her clients on the phone. So much for *her* emotions. She changed so fast, it made me want to vomit.

After hanging up, her smile melted.

"Did I say you could come out?" she said, not even looking at me.

"I'm starving. Can I eat dinner at least?"

"Dinner?" Mama said, pausing to think about it. Not a good sign. "I'm too tired to get dinner going. You can make yourself a tuna sandwich."

I ignored her suggestion and opened the freezer. Mama stored everything in the freezer, including our ant-ridden baked goods, in case they spoiled and we caught a flesh-eating virus or mad cookie disease.

I was wearing Thayer's bandanna and hadn't washed my hair in three days. Lately, I liked staying dirty.

Mama said, "Take off that sloppy hat. Don't you know it's bad luck wearing a hat in the house?"

"It's not a hat, Mama. It's a bandanna." I had even managed my own way of wearing it—not flopped over my head, like a boy, but pulled back like Dr. Calaban's glittery scarf.

"Don't get fresh with me," Mama said, pushing her sunglasses toward the bridge of her nose. Who wore sunglasses indoors? Rock stars and idiots, that's who. Mama refused to buy a regular pair of prescription lenses. She said they made her look like a bag lady.

I had totally forgotten about my split ends, which Thayer had dyed with a Sharpie pen. Then Mama tugged the bandanna off my head and saw his arts and crafts project.

"What happened to your hair?" she asked, inspecting every strand.

"Nothing," I said, jerking away from her. "Let go of me."

"It's not coming off," she said. "What is this? Paint?"

I could've lied and said: "We were making anti-war posters in civics class and my hair fell into the paint can." But I couldn't. I kept remembering how Mama and I used to be so close. I would tell her everything.

"It's marker," I said.

"You colored your hair with marker?"

I sighed. "No. Let me finish. Just listen to me for a minute."

"It's not coming out. My Lord. You'll have to cut it," she said. "I'll make an appointment at Aruj and see if they can squeeze you in tomorrow."

"Forget it. I'm not going. For your information, I'm trying to grow it out."

"It looks absolutely appalling. I'm not asking you again," she said.

"It's my hair. Don't tell me how to wear it."

"Unbelievable," she said. "Am I supposed to feel sorry for you? What have you been doing all day? I'm the only one who cleans around here."

She took off her glasses, flicked her gaze over the bandanna, then at me. "Here," she said, flinging it on the floor. "You'll understand when you're older."

"I'll never understand!" I screeched at her retreating back. "I'm not perfect like you."

Mama whirled around, the sunglasses clenched between her teeth. Then she launched into another speech about something new: my voice. Apparently, I was too "defensive" and "sharp." Not to mention angry.

I tried to tell her that it wasn't true, but I had a hard time convincing myself.

Union of the Senses

Dr. Calaban was late. I sat in her plant-infested office, watching the second hand spin around. I hadn't seen Thayer in days. Maybe he had been kidnapped by Martians. As a kid, he used to sit on the roof and "summon" them with his mind. He said UFOs are attracted to Florida because it's so flat.

The more I listened to his crazy rambling, the quieter my thoughts became. I couldn't've cared less about counting, as long as he kept talking to me. Without him, I staged imaginary conversations in my mind. He would laugh at my lame jokes. He would call me pretty.

I couldn't figure out if we were officially dating. Nobody in Miami went on "dates." They spent every waking minute at the mall. Sometimes they patrolled the Falls, a chain of outdoor stores equipped with palm trees and fluorescent tide pools. Or else Sunset Place, where skaters skulked around in doglike packs. Or the arcade, where they got drunk because nobody checked their IDs.

At school, Sharon Lubbitz was spreading rumors that Thayer had written a Trenchcoat Mafia–style letter, detailing his plans to blow up the school. Yeah, right. Thayer would've written it in Klingon.

Still, his disappearance was shady. I was mulling it over when Dr. Calaban finally materialized.

Maybe six minutes wasn't worth losing my cool, but I let her have it.

"I don't need Paxil anymore," I announced, checking out another African violet on her desk. Their dull green leaves were dusted with hairs. I reached out and stroked them.

She raised an eyebrow. "Really? So now you're the doctor."

"It's like you don't listen to me," I said, still stroking the furry plant. "When I complain, you just up my prescription. I quit taking it because it made me sick."

"When did you stop taking your medication?"

"A few days ago."

"And how do you feel?"

"Dizzy. And I'd get these electric shock sensations. Sometimes I was so sick, I just laid in bed, waiting for the dizziness to go away."

Her dark eyes flashed. "Frances, you should never go off medication without supervision. SSRIs, such as Paxil, work by adjusting the amount of serotonin in your brain. Paxil washes out very quickly, which can jolt your nervous system."

I couldn't absorb all this doctor talk.

"So what am I supposed to do?"

"I'd like you to try taking Paxil in smaller doses, tapering off for a week."

"You want me to go on meds again so I can get off them? That doesn't make any sense."

"It's your choice," she said.

"Then I choose to quit."

"Either way, I would like to continue meeting with you and discussing your progress. You might want to revisit this issue down the road. Medication won't cure OCD or any other anxiety disorder. At least we have no evidence of this. I want you to believe that you can cope with your anxiety on your own. You possess that inner strength."

I watched her blinking at me. Then she asked a game show question.

"Can you come up with an example of someone who you would call courageous?"

All this New Agey garbage was getting on my nerves. So I gave her a smartass answer. "The lion in *The Wizard of Oz*."

Her mouth twitched, holding back a smile. "You are joking with me, no?"

Dr. Calaban faded away. I tried to focus on her bone bracelet. I wondered if she ever went to funerals, what her life was like outside the loony bin, her shrink's office.

"I think this is the best decision," she said. "If you can go to school and do what you need to do, I won't push you into continuing your medication."

Dr. Calaban didn't know me. As far as she knew, I was just another wacko.

"There's this boy," I heard myself say. "He takes Ritalin off and on. The medicine makes him feel worse instead of better. It changes him inside."

"Frances, are you afraid that taking antidepressants will change you?"

"It's like, I see things a certain way and I don't want to lose that."

"What do you mean?"

"Like the way I draw."

"Would you consider yourself visually oriented? Can you focus on images and patterns pretty easily?"

"Sure. I do it all the time. Especially when I play my violin."

Dr. Calaban brightened. "So you draw and play music?"

"Not at the same time," I said.

She laughed so hard, I saw metal glinting in her molars. "Frances, I would like to give you one more test."

I groaned. "Not again."

"You might enjoy this one. It's a quiz for artists," she said, handing me another stupid number two pencil.

The test took five minutes to finish. It asked a

lot of questions that seemed to have nothing in common: When I drew a picture, did I work on several at once? Or one at a time? (I couldn't start another picture until the first was perfect.) Did time pass unnoticed while drawing? Or did it tick by slowly? (That's why I liked to draw. Time would slip away.) Did I like to have music playing while I drew? (Of course. Music was everything to me.)

When I finished, Dr. Calaban added up my score, whatever that meant. She said, "Ahhh!" with an exclamation point on the end.

"So this finally proves that I'm crazy," I told her.

"No, Frances. It means that the left and right side of your brain are divided almost equally. It's like your hands when you play the violin. They're doing two separate things at the same time."

This made absolutely no sense. "My brain is divided," I said.

"The human brain has two hemispheres," she explained. "The left is the center of logic. This side takes over when you're working out a math problem or playing music. The right side of the brain is more intuitive. It processes things like dreams. This side takes over when you're drawing. Most of us tend to favor one or the other. You are lucky to have a brain that jumps between both hemispheres easily."

I stared at her for a minute. "You mean there's nothing wrong with my head?"

"Nothing. This is your normal way of seeing the world."

Normal? There wasn't anything normal about me.

"It's almost as if you have two heads," said Dr. Calaban. "And you are balancing them without a problem."

I couldn't get over it. Here I was, trying to square everything away, when I was already balanced on the inside.

"For example, are you good at math?" she asked.

"Not really. Doing math takes, like, forever."

"Why is that?"

"Because some numbers are lucky or unlucky."

Dr. Calaban mulled this over. "Do you have a special number that brings you luck?"

I clamped my mouth shut, prepared to sit there in silence. But ever since I'd been talking to Thayer, it didn't seem so weird sharing with Dr. Calaban.

"Yeah, I have a special number," I admitted. "It changes all the time. I used to switch the lights on and off three times or something bad would happen to my family. If I messed up, I thought they would die."

"But they didn't."

"No," I said. "And something bad happened anyway."

"The divorce?"

"Yeah."

Dr. Calaban leaned forward. "Frances, how is tapping a light switch going to keep your family safe? Think about it. Does this make any sense?"

No, it didn't.

"If you think that's bad, you should see my mom." I rolled my eyes. "She checks the locks, like, fifteen times a day."

Dr. Calaban was quiet for a moment. "How do you feel about this?"

"I'm used to it. After the move, she's been worse."

"What do you mean 'worse'?"

"She doesn't want me going anywhere on my

own, but she won't drive me, either. She doesn't even want me to get a learner's permit. Before we leave the house, she checks to make sure the stove is off, as if we're going to burn down the house or something."

"And what sort of rituals did you have after the move?"

"Lots of things. Like when I do my homework, everything has to be in order. I have to count and sharpen all my pencils, whether they need it or not. Sometimes it takes hours just to do one assignment."

"Is this any different from your mother's rituals?"

I blinked. "You mean, it's possible that my mom has OCD too?" I asked. My mind raced back to all her cleaning routines: the paper garbage bags in the kitchen, her purse crammed with Ziploc bags, everything squared away. I always found it strange, but I wouldn't have called it a "ritual," not like my number-counting obsession.

It made sense. All this time, I had been trying to fit my imaginary rules into some kind of order, a system to chase away the crazy feelings. And here,

Dr. Calaban was giving me a logical explanation, not only for my rituals, but for Mama's as well.

"Yes, it's possible," said Dr. Calaban. "What do you believe?"

I believed she was right.

The Order of Things

It was a year after we moved to Miami. Numbers didn't mean much to me yet. They were marks on my flash cards, Morse code. Then my parents walked into my brand-new bedroom with their mouths stretched as tight as minus signs.

We need to talk, they said.

I was sitting on my bed, reading. "What's going on?" I asked.

Dad opened his mouth. Out came the words. This is what I heard:

"Your mother and I have decided not to stay together. We are separating from each other, but this doesn't mean that we're abandoning you or that we don't love you anymore."

In my book, the pictures faded, as if Dad had

turned down the tint in my head.

Dad said: "Be good to your mother." The softness in his voice pricked my eyes. It was getting hard to breathe. Dad sat next to me. He was wearing his 9-to-5 threads: suspenders and a suit ironed so sharply I could open mail with the creases. Up close, I could see his pasty scalp.

I tried to focus on my astronomy book. I dragged my finger over Saturn's rings like the grooves on a record and started counting the silence. I flopped on the floor, heaving great, phlegmy sobs. Mama hauled me into an embrace. She was saying something, but I couldn't make out the words. All I heard were the numbers banging inside me. I looked at Dad and saw him with another wife. She would scowl at my bottle-cap collection, the overdue library books under my bed. She would try to scold me and I wouldn't listen.

The next day, Mama dragged me to the mall. At the cosmetics counter, a lady let me try expensive perfume that she said was so grown up. I sprayed some on my wrist and couldn't stop spraying. I had to keep spraying until it felt like the right number of times. I ducked into the restroom and tried to wash it off. The ugly smell didn't go away. For the rest of the afternoon, I tried to ignore it, but it stuck like a splinter in my mind.

When I got home, I ran upstairs and turned on the bath. I filled the tub until it overflowed. I dunked my head. I wanted to stay underwater until all the air trickled out of me. I held my breath, counting seconds of quiet.

Mama freaked out and made me clean up the tiles. I spent an hour mopping it with wet towels. But it wasn't good enough. Finally, Mama shooed me away and finished the job, though I think bleaching the floor was going a little overboard.

Then I developed a washing routine. This was something I always used to do as a little kid. But now it was getting out of control. If I messed up—shampooing my hair first—I'd have to start over. Unfortunately, the order kept changing and I couldn't remember how to do it right.

I started collecting all kinds of things—twigs, bottle caps, wire. My room grew piles in every corner. I saved Coke cans and stacked them in the garage. I shoved a shoebox under my bed. I crammed it with my favorite things: a hunk of brain coral, a bag tinkling with silver dollars won at a snow-shoveling contest.

Mama told me to clean my room, but things had to be done in a certain order. She would remake my bed after I'd tucked in the corners. I looked down at my hands, rubbed raw from counting, and didn't know what to do with them.

Lint Pickers

Mama pulled into the driveway and I hopped out. Within seconds, they were all over me—mosquitoes dotting my arms like thumbtacks. I smeared them off, but a new swarm took over like instant reincarnation. The city sent trucks to poison them. Fog would soak the yard and cloud the windowpane. They sent planes that soared so low, the house rattled. Still, the black spots bounced against the windowpane, bringing zombie movies to mind.

"Fin, would you like to wash the car for me?" Mama asked. She was already rattling around in the closet, pulling out a bucket.

No, I wouldn't like to wash the car while billions of bloodsucking insects made me their pincushion.

But Mama made it clear I had no choice.

Washing the car was a blast with Dad. He taught me the proper technique. Always start at the top. The side facing the sun came last since it dried the quickest.

Toweling off the car turned into a ritual—one that chilled me out. I stretched the rag—one of Dad's old T-shirts—and pulled it over the roof, squeezed out the water, rinsed the windows. I would dry the whole car in the same order. I doubted that anyone got such a thrill from washing a car.

Once, I asked Dad how to change a tire. Mama wouldn't let me try. "Too dangerous. One slip and she'll crush her foot," she said.

"You've got to be kidding," Dad said. Even he thought Mama was crazy.

I watched Dad demonstrate and that was my tire-changing lesson, standing at a distance.

After I finished rinsing, Mama came and inspected it. Of course, it wasn't clean enough.

"What's this smudge on the bumper?" she asked, scraping the white streak with her pointy fingernails.

"It's a scratch. It doesn't come off," I said.

"You scratched the car?"

I counted to three and said, "No. It's been there since we moved. Probably some whack-ass Miami driver."

"Don't use that kind of language around me, young lady."

"What kind?"

She shot me a look. "Are you going to help me or not?"

"Why bother fixing it? You never drive anywhere except school and the grocery store."

"Quit giving me static," she said.

I rubbed three times and the scratch wouldn't vanish. Mama snatched the cloth away and tried. I left her there, rubbing circles into the bumper.

When I stepped inside the house, I smelled something burning. Mama had left a saucepan on the stove, scorching up butter. You'd think that she would've noticed, after checking and rechecking every plugged-in appliance. I dumped the pan in the sink, cranked the faucet until it sizzled. Then I turned up the air-conditioning.

The stink had crept into my jeans. No use washing them. I had an urge to stuff them in the trash. Instead, I shoved them under my bed, along with the bags of bottle caps. I needed new clothes. Nothing I wore made any sense here. My T-shirts were thermal. My prettiest tops were sweaters with pom-poms.

I could picture myself at fifty, bitching about the weather, wearing pearls and a skirt that dragged on the ground. Right now, the only nonembarrassing thing in my closet was a pair of too-white sneakers. Thayer and I had decorated them with Sharpie pens. This took place in class, when he drew a heart on both soles. I added wings so my feet could fly. We kept doodling, but only on the bottom. Otherwise Mama would notice. She would say that I had ruined the shoes and, therefore, wasted her hard-earned money.

Lying on my bed, I heard mosquitoes whine and hover. Ducking under the covers didn't help. They could smell me breathing. Their bites stung like a flu shot. I got used to carrying Kleenex and wiping off the blood. My blood.

Mama was a Kleenex freak. She tucked folded sheets into her waistband. Who took the time to fold Kleenex? I was forever finding trampled sheets on the bathroom floor. I figured that she draped the toilet seat with tissue to avoid contact with germs. The fact that this had crossed my mind was proof of my insanity. No doubt, it was genetic.

I lit a candle to cover up the stink of my jeans, put on a fresh pair, then headed back to the kitchen and poured a bowl of cereal. That was all my queasy stomach could tolerate. On top of the box was Dad's "copy," his stupid paragraphs about healthy hearts and granola. Out of all the organic crap Mama could've bought, why did she pick Dad's brand? I pondered this unsolved mystery while dumping in a healthy splash of chocolate milk. Dad was the only human I knew (besides me) who ate cereal 24/7. I'd find him poking around the cupboard in the middle of the night, searching for a clean spoon or a cup. Once, I caught him eating cornflakes out of a wooden salad bowl at 2 a.m.

"Don't tell your mother," he had whispered, making sure to rinse the bowl and put it back just the way he'd found it. She always figured it out anyway. Unless Mama scrubbed a dish herself, it was never clean enough.

I carried the bowl back to my room—a major no-no, eating where a crumb might fall on the carpet and stain it for life. I put the bowl on my bed. I had the urge to leave and stand in the hallway, so I did. Of course, this made no sense. I counted to three and tapped the wall, feeling like a computer with a virus. Error. Please restart. I was back on my bed, slurping the last chocolaty drop, when Mama barged in.

"Something burning?" she said, wrinkling her nose.

"Yeah. Our dinner," I said.

Mama stood there, sniffing like a bloodhound. "It's freezing in here. Did you touch the air conditioner?"

"Yes, I touched it. And I also turned it on."

"Don't get fresh with me," she said. "The electric bill is going to be sky-high this month. I have the gauge set on seventy-two. It must stay on that number. Understand?"

I nodded. Seven and two were odd and even.

Definitely not friends.

She looked at the empty bowl. "Were you eating in here? You know that's not allowed. And why are you eating so close to dinner?"

Then she did something that sent me over the edge. She stepped out of the room, as if testing the air quality of the hallway, and came back and sat on my bed. This meant that she had entered my room twice. In a flash, I pictured her dying in the hospital, all because she hadn't obeyed my ritual of threes.

"Mama, please get out," I blurted, much louder than I had intended.

"Excuse me?" Mama said. She didn't move.

I subtracted two from seven, super fast, inside my head. It didn't work. When I started whispering, Mama turned and gave me a look that said: *You've lost it.*

"Can you leave for a second and come back?" I asked.

She glared. "Fin, what has gotten into you?"

The number two. That's what.

I needed three to keep her safe. My rituals had become so big, I was asking Mama to perform them too.

Mama ignored me. She rushed over to my candle—a twenty-three-ounce jar of Dreamsicle Bay—and blew it out. "I thought the house was on fire. Look at all that smoke," she said. "That's a cheap wick. Did you know that candles leak dangerous levels of lead into the air?"

Here we go again.

I glanced up and saw a mosquito glued to her forehead. Mama wouldn't smack it, though she worried about West Nile all the time. She never killed bugs, not even moths, which she'd cup with her bare hands and fling outside. They'd probably die after losing the dust on their wings. Mama said I'd go blind if the dust got in my eyes. I didn't believe her, but their squishy bodies freaked me out.

She kept talking and I couldn't focus. All I could see was that bloodsucking bug on her face. So I reached over and shooed it off. I shooed two more times, although the bug had gone. I needed to make it even.

Mama snatched my wrist. "Stop touching me," she said.

"There was something gross on your face," I

said. That didn't come out right.

"Are you trying to be funny?"

"No," I said.

"When was the last time you washed this sweater?" she asked, picking a speck of lint off my sleeve. If I had noticed, I would've beat her to it. When she did it again, I saw they were paint flakes, not lint. Let's talk about the dangerous levels of lead in paint.

Now I had to scrub the mosquito germs from my hands. I headed toward the door. She dodged in front of it, cornering me.

"Mama, I can't breathe," I shouted. "I need space."

"You have a bedroom all to yourself," she said. "Most teenage girls would be grateful."

"What teenage girls? I haven't met them."

"Why don't you come outside and take a walk with me?" she asked. "It's a nice day."

"It's hot. And the mosquitoes are wicked."

Mama said, "Fine. You can stay in here."

I didn't consider this a jail sentence.

At exactly six o'clock, she heated TV dinners in

a plastic tray: the kind that came with three different triangular compartments. Since triangles added up to good luck, I had no problem chowing down on Salisbury steak, lumpy potatoes, and frozen peas, as long as the stuff didn't touch.

If Dr. Calaban took notes on my eating habits, she'd think we lived in a trailer. Mama and I weren't exactly living the high life after the divorce, but we weren't surviving off food stamps, either. Mama just couldn't care less about cooking. She'd rather nuke a microwave dinner than plan a meal with the basic food groups. Was it four or five? I couldn't remember. Those weren't my numbers anyway.

My eyes darted around the room. I could still smell the burned saucepan, my cancerous candle, paint fumes, mosquito blood, and moth dust. There was lint in my lungs, knitting its way through my throat. Living here was a health hazard. Sooner or later, we were going to get sick.

Prismacolor

When I saw Dr. Calaban, she said, "You look thin." Sure, I had lost weight. At this point, I could pull off my jeans without unbuttoning them. Still, she acted like I had a choice in this no-food diet. In fact, I couldn't eat anything when my blood was full of leftover Paxil and burbling like it might erupt. My mouth tasted like metal. Even swallowing grossed me out. Maybe quitting wasn't such a good idea.

I didn't tell her about this.

"Frances, why do you believe that your mother brought you here?"

Dr. Calaban kept quiet.

I fiddled with a loose thread on my sock. "Mama thinks I'm traumatized by the divorce. I can't stand to be around her for extended lengths of time. She even stopped asking me about Thayer."

"Thayer?"

I quit messing with my sock. Oh, God. Now I had mentioned his name, one of her own patients.

"Thayer's this boy I know."

She waited. I looked at her wrist, but I didn't see the bone bracelet.

"We're just friends."

She scribbled in her notes.

"We hang out a lot. He's teaching me how to do graf."

She shook her head. "I don't know this word."

I thought about the buildings downtown, the tags we had left there. "Graffiti gives my hands something to do besides counting. It's fun." On the inside of my arm were three letters, FIN, which I had perfected in felt tip, the edges trimmed with stars. It was time I made my own tag. I held it up for Dr. Calaban to see. At first, I thought she might laugh.

She leaned closer. "Tell me what else you do for fun."

"Draw, I guess."

"That's right. And before you moved, what did you like to do in Vermont? Did you play any sports?"

"Well, I used to go horseback riding. It was like being in another world. I could totally zone out, you know?"

Dr. Calaban smiled. She had this huge gap between her front teeth that I could've poked a pencil through.

When we moved, Mama promised I could find another stable and continue my lessons. That didn't happen. I had a feeling she wanted me to quit. She said I'd fall off and break my neck. I could see Mama standing near the horse stalls waiting for me, pretending to do her crossword puzzle while the girls with the French braids stared and giggled.

I rode for three years in a row. Not once did I fall off.

Dr. Calaban pulled out a box of Prismacolors and paper and told me to draw.

"What is this? Art class?" I said, reaching for a pencil labeled "salmon." This would've come in handy back in kindergarten, when I couldn't find the right shade for people as sun challenged as me. For some reason, all the other kids used orange, which didn't cut it for me.

Last week, we had tried relaxation exercises to help me with my so-called nervous habits. Dr. Calaban's voice swirled around me, saying things like "Imagine your feet are getting heavier and warmer," as if I had put on a pair of lead boots. We moved up from my toes to my fingers, but it never felt like the right order. Finally, she quit when I fell asleep in the chair.

Dr. Calaban said, "I asked if you wanted to play a game. You didn't seem too thrilled with cards or checkers."

"I hate board games," I told her. They were called "bored games" for a reason.

"Fine," she said. "But you've often mentioned that you love to draw. Did you know that I also draw?"

I put down the salmon pencil. "For real?" I said.

"Actually, I like to paint on the weekends," she said, smiling.

This was too much. Dr. Calaban, the artiste? I

tried to picture her spidery legs under a paint-stained smock, along with her weaponlike heels.

"I feel stupid trying to sketch with this thing in my lap," I said. "Can I sit on the floor? Or is that too weird?"

"Do whatever makes you feel comfortable," she said, tightening her scarf.

For once, I didn't feel like a freak crouched in that chair with her eyes locked on me. I spread out on the carpet, arranging my colored pencils in perfect rows like the numbers in my solar system. When I did stuff like this, I wasn't aware of it half the time. I felt like a robot on autopilot.

Dr. Calaban was still blabbing away, but I wasn't listening. Her mouth opened and closed. I had never seen a brighter lipstick. It was the kind worn by television stars, not normal people.

"Art is therapeutic. Sometimes we become entrenched in the emotional experience of a dilemma. Drawing allows you to express yourself without words," said Dr. Calaban.

I fixed my gaze on the blank sheet of paper. "What am I supposed to draw?" I asked.

"I want you to sketch something that represents

who you are," she said. Then she did something that threw me off guard. She slid out from behind her desk and knelt on the floor next to me.

After a while, we sketched in silence. I concentrated on shading. It was easy tuning out everything around me—the air conditioner's hum, sunlight dribbling through the blinds, voices chuckling in the hall, my stomach rumbling for no reason. I snuck a peek at her sketch pad. I expected lollipop trees and stick figures. Instead, she drew her own naked brown foot (no longer crammed into the pointy stilettos).

"That is majorly impressive," I said. "Feet are difficult to draw. Mine always turn out like flippers."

I kept staring at her paper. Her intricate doodle looked just like the real deal. She didn't need fancy supplies. Dr. Calaban dragged a ballpoint pen across her legal pad, the lines bisecting her doodle, just like Mama's "grid-transfer" method.

Even more surprising was her foot itself. I had always suspected that Dr. Calaban treated herself to weekly pedicures, most likely choosing a violent shade of red polish. But her toenails gleamed even without polish, the edges trim, yet uneven. No doubt a do-it-yourself job hidden inside those fancy shoes.

"Thanks," she said. "So tell me about your drawing."

I knew this was a trap.

"It doesn't mean anything," I said. So there.

"You're right. It doesn't have to mean anything," she said.

I sighed. "That's what I hated about art class."

"I thought you were taking orchestra?"

"I am. This was back in Vermont. My art teacher was obsessed with public speaking. We had to stand in front of the class and explain why we drew a unicorn or whatever."

"And how did you feel about that?" she asked.

"Stupid. I mean, what a waste of time. Why can't art mean different things to different people? Why should it mean the same thing to everybody? It's like asking us to see the world the same way, which is impossible."

Dr. Calaban leaned back and studied her drawing. "Would you want to live in that kind of world?"

"Of course not," I said. "It's like the people at school. Everybody's so fake."

"How so?" she asked.

"From the minute you start school, you're fed a bunch of lies: Be yourself. Don't follow the crowd, blah blah. What they really mean is: Follow the crowd. Just make sure that it's the right one."

"And if you don't?" Dr. Calaban raised her eyebrows at me.

"Suffer the consequences," I said.

My drawing hadn't turned out the way I wanted. Stuck in the middle of the paper was this knobby-looking horse in a forest of skyscrapers. I shaded a line of thick, soft lead across the bottom, as if paving a road. Now the animal's hooves appeared bolted into the ground.

Dr. Calaban squinted at my work. "How do you feel about this drawing?"

I chewed my lip. "I hate how this horse looks. I wish I could rip her out of the picture."

"Why is that?" Dr. Calaban asked.

"So she could be free."

We both looked at each other.

Dr. Calaban crumpled her paper and threw it in the trash can. "I think that's good for now," she said, rising and smoothing her skirt.

"That was a nice drawing. Why toss it?" I asked.

"Because I can always do another," she said.

"That's so odd," I told her. "For me, drawing is always about finishing a piece."

"And do you always take the time to finish them?" Dr. Calaban asked. She was back at her desk, in business mode again.

"See, I could spend days perfecting a doodle in the corner of my math book," I said.

"Except it never looks perfect," she said.

"Yeah." I nodded. "So true."

Dr. Calaban smiled. I was actually beginning to like her. So I made a promise to myself. I would try a little harder to open up.

"Listen," she said. "I have a homework assignment for you."

"I don't need more homework," I said. I had enough trouble finishing my math worksheets on a nightly basis.

"Here's your assignment. Whenever you feel

like counting, I want you to take out your drawing supplies and concentrate on that instead. Can you handle that?"

"Deal," I said.

"What are you going to do with today's drawing?" she wanted to know.

As I folded the paper into quarters, I could feel her waiting to see what I'd do next.

"I'm taking it home," I said.

Useless One

Mama never drove in the rain. After school, I saw the Nissan parked under a tree, the windshield flecked with sparkling droplets.

"Let's go. Hurry," Mama said as I slid into my seat. "The weather's getting nasty."

She spent the entire ride home talking about water spouts and sinkholes, all of which were spotted in Miami during the last five minutes, according to the Weather Channel.

"That's just hype, Mama," I said. "It's not even raining hard."

"This is only the start of it," she said, ultra-serious.

I laughed and she pinched my arm.

"Ouch. Quit it," I said.

"You better straighten up, young lady. I'm getting sick of this attitude," she said.

I was already sick of hers.

As we turned onto Useless One (otherwise known as US 1), passing a Honda throbbing with bass, I noticed a pair of chewed-looking Keds dangling from a power line.

"Do you think there're gangs around here?" I asked.

"Of course not. This is a nice neighborhood," said Mama.

"How do you know? I mean, there's a lot going on that we don't notice," I said.

"Mmm," said Mama. She turned on the radio and hit scan.

"I mean, don't you ever wonder if the stars in the sky are really there or if—"

"Hush, Fin. I'm trying to hear this," she said, as an announcer came on and read the news in a dead monotone, just the way Sharon and her dumb friends read the morning announcements at school. *"Somebody was blown up in some country. And today's lunch special is tater tots."*

When we got home, I left the drawing on the kitchen counter, hoping that Mama would find it and say something like, "Wow. This is really good. I didn't know you could draw so well."

I took a long bath, just sitting in the tub, thinking. My head buzzed like a cassette tape on fast forward. I got a whiff of our leftovers burning behind the door. We'd probably end up eating sandwiches again at the rate Mama was going.

I got out and toweled off my hair. The tips were still black, almost touching my shoulders now. No more mophead. Or as Thayer called it, a Purdey cut, like Emma Peel, the bad-ass chick on that old-school TV show, *The Avengers*. Even my eyebrows were thickening back into place.

As I shrugged into my robe, I pretended it was a crime-fighting catsuit. I cocked my fingers like a gun and aimed for the light switch.

"Mrs. Peel . . . we are needed," I whispered.

Mama began knocking. "Blah blah . . . Wasting water . . . ," she said.

I flung open the door and brushed past her in a cloud of steam.

She brandished a can of low-sodium soup. "We're having a cleansing meal."

I groaned.

"Do you want creamy tomato or chicken noodle?" she asked.

"Neither," I said. That fat-free, condensed stuff made me want to hurl.

"I'll use milk instead of water, just like your father did," she said.

"That's okay." I was rooting around in the cupboard looking for the can opener. Besides food, our kitchen lacked the basic cooking gadgets. Once, I caught Mama straining soup through the diamond-shaped hole she had cut with a can punch.

Not only was Dad the designated cook in the house, he was also its emotional thermostat. Mama, the hard-hitting fact finder, only showed her feelings when she was upset with me. Lately this seemed like an ongoing event.

I turned to the kitchen counter. "Where's the piece of paper that I left here?" I asked, digging through yogurt lids and Chinese menus speckled with crusty stains.

Mama frowned. "What paper? I'm always picking up your papers."

"Oh, right. I forgot," I said, rolling my eyes. "Always." I went back to searching the cupboard.

"Frances, don't raise your voice," she said.

"I'm raising my voice because I'm frustrated," I said, banging the cupboard shut. "I can't leave anything around without you throwing it out. You don't even ask."

"If I didn't clean up, we'd have a mess," she said, reaching into the trash. "Is this it?"

"Yeah," I said. Gross. I couldn't touch the paper after it had sat in garbage, even if it had just rested on top.

"So, why are you standing there? Take it," she said.

I gritted my teeth. "It's dirty now."

"What's gotten into you?" she asked, cramming the paper into my fist. "I feel as if we're having this constant power struggle and I'd like it to stop."

I unfolded the drawing. The top left corner looked soggy. Before I knew what I was doing, I tore it off.

Mama watched me rip away the background until nothing was left but the mare I had drawn in the middle.

"I didn't think you drew anymore," she said.

I threw the scraps in the trash and washed my hands, then headed straight for my room. As I locked the door, I realized how barren it seemed, not counting the wing-shaped finger stains near the doorknob. I decided to Scotch tape my drawing to the door.

Standing back, I surveyed my work. The horse wasn't stuck in the ground anymore. Without the buildings behind her, she could've stood anywhere, getting ready to run.

D	E	C	E	M	B	E	R
4	5	3	5	13	2	5	18

Archaeological Evidence

t's official," Thayer said. "I'm now the oldest kid in our class."

When I saw him leaning against my locker at lunchtime, I wanted to choke him. He was fiddling with his tape recorder again, hitting the "play" button on and off so Ms. Armstrong's week-old lecture on plate tectonics resembled a complicated rap anthem.

"I haven't seen you in centuries," I said, struggling to balance my violin case. God, I sounded obnoxious. "I mean, I heard you got suspended."

"I've been hella busy," he said, rubbing his nose.

"Doing what?" I asked.

"Getting suspended," he said.

"For smoking?"

He glared. "No. For skipping a Saturday detention."

I almost laughed. "Why did you do that?"

"Because I forgot."

Classroom doors slammed. Jocks prowled the hall, grunting and swearing. Sharon's high-pitched giggle floated above the noise.

Thayer said, "Let's make like a tree and leave."

We couldn't hide in the music room anymore, not after Mr. Clemmons had caught us eating there, so we met in the grassy clearing behind the science lab, on a marble bench beside a stranger's memorial.

"I'm almost the same age as her." Thayer brushed off the slab. "This girl died, like, a decade ago."

"What happened?"

"A car crash. She was at the wheel, drunk. Can you guess why she gets a memorial?"

"No. Why?"

"Who the hell knows?"

"I bet her family had a ton of money," I said, reaching into my backpack and finding my pencil box. Inside was the mangled jigsaw of Ms. Armstrong's trombone-playing son. I sprinkled the pieces over the memorial. They fluttered at odd angles, cartwheeling into the weeds.

Thayer pulled out his pipe. I couldn't believe he had the nerve to smoke at school, much less an illegal substance. No wonder he had been held back.

"Happy birthday," I told him.

"Muchas gracias," he said. "So where's my present?"

I wasn't sure if he was joking. His stare was making me nervous, so I changed the subject.

"There's nothing historic to see in Miami."

"Except me," he said, coughing.

"You'd be lucky to find a fifty-year-old building. And they'd probably knock it down and build a giant condo."

"You don't really know this city," he said. "I understand why you hate it here. But you have to look a little harder."

"For what?"

"Mysteries." He stood. "Come on."

"Where?"

"You'll never guess."

I could hear people laughing, talking on their

221

way to class. "We have to get back."

"Says who? Oh, ye of little faith."

Not for the first time, I was ditching Ms. Armstrong's lecture on forces and motion to ride the Metrorail downtown, a half-hour ride from my house. One moment I was a hostage at Miami Dade High, and the next I was on a bridge with Thayer.

Mama would flip if she knew I used public transportation. I associated it with germs. She associated it with thieves and rapists.

We stood near a construction site, looking down at a smattering of holes. The Miami Circle. Or, as Thayer would suggest, a landing pad for spaceships.

Just a few years ago, a real estate mogul was going to build a million-dollar condo on the banks of the Miami River. When the old apartments on the site were demolished, archaeologists swooped in and discovered the holes chiseled into bedrock.

How had the Circle remained undiscovered for so long? The site lay buried beneath rusty pipes and slabs of cement. So far, the archaeologists had dug up thousands of artifacts: beads and bones.

"I saw this psychic on TV," Thayer said. "She

thinks the Tequestas made human sacrifices here."

"Tequestas?"

"The People of the Glades."

Now the sun had slipped behind a clump of gleaming skyscrapers. We walked closer. Thayer was sweating in his army jacket. He peeled it off, exposing his pale shoulders.

"I know how to get over the fence," he said.

I snorted. "Yeah, like I'm going down there."

Still, I followed him out through the parking garage.

We stepped outside and stood on the root-buckled sidewalk. I watched an iguana scuttle through the sawgrass, its tail whipping.

"Iguanas eat flowers," Thayer told me.

The bottom of the Circle was pecked with gaps. Thayer dubbed it "Valley of the Holes." The archaeologists had left little flags raised like exclamation points. He wedged his feet into the chain-link fence and scurried up.

"Hurry," he urged.

"Are you crazy?"

He hit the ground. I could hear him breathing

hard. Thayer ran to the Circle and, a couple of minutes later, returned with his prize—a flat piece of stone, thin as a splinter.

"It's cool," he said. "Everything's cool."

He climbed the fence again and dangled there, silent. Then he took out the stone, holding it up for me to see.

"You stole that?" I said. Could I sound any dumber?

Thayer tossed it to me. "Anyone who holds it must speak their mind. If you don't, it will heat up and burn a hole through your skin."

I didn't like where this was headed. I threw it back. He caught it one-handed. "Who's got it now?" I said, trying to laugh.

"Okay, okay." He closed his eyes. "I'm thirsty."

I laughed for real. "No fair."

He pressed the stone between his eyebrows. "I want to see . . . something I've never seen."

"I don't know," I said. "Is that possible?"

"It's my birthday. I can do whatever I want. That is, if you're up for the challenge."

I looked away. The Circle was amazing. I loved that he shared it with me. "I'm up for it."

He smirked. "Nah. You couldn't show me anything I haven't already explored."

"You better give me that stone."

"As you wish," he said.

We rode the Metrorail along US 1, from Brickell down to Dadeland South station. Tourists think the Metrorail works like a subway, only aboveground. This is mostly true, except the Metrorail doesn't take you anywhere convenient. You get off at Bayside mall, but you still have to walk a mile to the entrance, which kind of defeats the purpose of public transportation.

I decided to bring Thayer to the empty house. My neighborhood was just a short walk from the station, across from a vacant lot, the only one left. Everywhere we looked were McMansions that could've dropped from the sky—like Dorothy's house in *The Wizard of Oz*.

I got off the train and clomped down the stairs. We dodged the honking, swerving sea of cars on South Dixie Highway and raced through the parking lot of Pollo Tropical. Finally we slipped into the gridlike suburban avenues of Pinecrest, all numbers, no names. You can't even cut through people's backyards, thanks to the chain-link fences and concrete walls. Not to mention block after block of "gated communities."

"So you live around here? Where's your house?" Thayer asked.

"I live a few miles south," I said, not wanting to share more. "Usually I ride my bike to the station."

He nodded. "You live in one of these chichi villages?"

"No. Gated communities suck. They're like apartment buildings with doormen who block you from walking into the lobby. Instead, they block you from walking on the sidewalk."

"It's the fortress mentality," Thayer said.

When we reached the empty house, Thayer hopped over the fence, ignoring the NO TRESPASSING signs. A busted lock dangled from a chain. Thayer stuffed the lock in his bag. What he'd do with it I couldn't tell.

I trooped toward the door, which was swung open so wide, you could herd camels through it.

Thayer whistled. "How did you find this joint?"

He didn't wait for my answer. "Man, I could blow the wall with tags."

I lifted the sofa pillow and took out my pills.

"You might want to get a couple fat Pilot markers," Thayer said, not paying attention. "Practice tagging. Especially letters. Patterns and fades aren't as important."

I tallied the leftover pills. Lost count, started again.

"Yo, where'd you get the candy?" he said.

"It's mine."

He coughed four times. "No shit?"

I passed him the bottle.

"Paxil, huh? I forget. How long you been eating it?"

"Since the beginning of school."

"Is this why you've been seeing the Bone Lady?"

"What?"

"That's what I call Dr. Calaban."

"Oh." I smiled. "Yeah, she's got that weird bracelet. Maybe it's a good luck charm."

Thayer rolled his eyes. "I don't believe in luck."

"Really?"

"There's nothing you can do about it. Whatever happens isn't good or bad. It's just what's meant to be." His gaze met mine.

"It's taken me a while to figure that out."

"For real?" He moved so close, I got a whiff of smoke. There was nothing left to do but spill.

"Listen. I have this . . . obsession . . . with numbers. I need to count things to feel in control. I've been doing it all my life, but it's gotten much worse lately."

"You have OCD?" He said it so matter-of-factly.

"It sounds dumb, right? I thought Paxil would help me get over it. But it made me sick. So I quit. Only it's like . . . the drug hasn't left my body."

"No shit?"

"You think I'd make this up? Besides, I still have the stone."

"Left or right pocket?" he said.

"Um. Left, I think."

He slid his hand inside my pocket. "Now it's my turn."

"Wait," I said. "If you use it too much, the stone loses its power."

He stepped back. "Okay. You can keep it for now," he said in a quiet voice.

"Thanks for hearing me out."

"No problem. It's good you quit the meds."

"I hope so."

"But you should've tapered off slowly," he added.

"Dr. Calaban said I might need antidepressants for the rest of my life. I thought they were training wheels, something to change my perspective so I could deal on my own."

"Who says you need to change your perspective? Maybe OCD is like perfect rhythm. It's in you, right? I think you can learn to roll with it. You don't need that Paxil garbage banging around your cranium."

Just mentioning Paxil made my head buzz.

I could still feel the heat from Thayer's fist warming my pocket. I'd told him about my freak-ishness and he hadn't run away. What's more, he seemed to get it. My obsessions belonged to me, for better or worse.

Once we got back to school, nothing was different. I waited on the bench, looking for

Mama's car. Thayer rolled off with a noisy pack of skaters. I didn't recognize any of them, so I guessed they went to another school. I waved but he didn't wave back. I took out the stone, another crumbly hunk of coral for my collection. I pitched it in the road. Two seconds later, I decided to go back and get it.

Standing there, kicking the pebbles around, I realized that all the rocks looked the same. I couldn't be sure if I had picked the right one, not that it mattered so much. I grabbed the flattest piece of coral and shoved it in my pocket. Then I remembered to breathe.

Secrets

I was tired of keeping secrets.

I came home from school and sniffed Raid hanging like a cloud in the air, and found the kitchen in shambles. Mama was on "ant patrol" again, ripping the cabinets off their hinges.

"They're everywhere," she muttered. "I can't seem to get rid of them."

She had tried cucumber sprays and ant traps, not to mention every bug repellent known to man. They came back in droves, popping up in my cereal bowl, floating in the milk like punctuation marks.

While putting back the groceries, stacking cans in Mama's preordained order (soup up front, tuna in the back), I asked, "Do you ever think about Dad?"

She slid her eyes across the kitchen. Maybe she

had been waiting for this question.

"It's perfectly normal to miss him," she said.

This wasn't really an answer.

I said, "Dr. Calaban and I have been talking a lot."

"That's good," she said, folding a paper bag to reuse later. She kept creasing the corners until they were straight.

"She thinks I have obsessive-compulsive disorder."

Mama shoved the folded bag behind the refrigerator. "Oh, we all have that to some degree." She laughed a little.

"It's not a joke," I said.

She didn't turn around.

"This disease is controlling my life and I want it to stop," I said. "Dr. Calaban says it tends to run in families. It's, like, genetic or something. Do you know anything about this?"

"Oh, gosh, Fin," she said. "Your grandmother used to wash her hands over and over. That was her thing."

"Well, my thing is counting," I said. I didn't tell

her that hand washing was my thing too.

"You mean, like a magic number?" she asked.

"Yes." That was it exactly.

"It will go away on its own. You have to be strong and say, 'I won't let it bother me anymore.' That's what I did. I mean, when I was a lot younger."

That was it? Just tell it to go away? Did she really know what it felt like, living under an evil spell, following the rules and never feeling in control? I couldn't believe that she had anything in common with me, despite our DNA.

"Did you ever try medication?" I asked.

Mama was rearranging the fridge now, clinking bottles. "That's not your business," she said.

"It *is* my business. You gave this to me. Now I have to deal with it."

"Fin, I don't want to discuss it anymore."

"But I do."

She slammed the refrigerator door. "My physician gave me belladonna. It's a homeopathic remedy. He said it would calm my nerves. I didn't know any better back then."

I considered the word "belladonna," tasting it on my tongue until it made no sense. It sounded like an evil princess in a fairy tale. "Did it help?" I asked.

"In the beginning, yes. Then I couldn't stand it," she said.

I clenched my fists behind my back. Opened them. Clenched again. "What do you mean, 'couldn't stand it'?"

"I didn't like the way it made me feel. Detached. Like I was dreaming all the time and couldn't wake up."

I nodded. I knew how that felt, sleeping while awake, everything at a distance.

"So I stopped taking it. I got really sick, Fin. I laid in bed for days, just shaking. I thought I was going to die. Then I finally told the doctor and he tapered me off slowly. But I will never go back on it again."

"When was this?" I asked.

"Please, Fin. I don't want to keep talking about it."

"When?" I repeated.

"After you were born," she said, looking at the floor.

I shoved my finger in my mouth and chewed the ragged edges. I'd said that Mama had given OCD to me, passing it down through our genes like dirty blond hair and skinny hips. Now it seemed the other way around.

"Was I a bad baby?" I asked, my voice cracking.

Mama folded her arms around me, squeezing so hard, my ribs ached. I could feel her pulse thumping out of sync with mine. She smelled the same as always—Ivory soap and cigarettes.

"You were a delightful baby," she said. "Your face lit up whenever someone walked into the room. You would stretch out your arms, asking to be held."

"I did?" I said. This was hard to believe.

"But taking care of you was a lot of work. You never wanted to sleep. I wasn't prepared for it," she said.

Even as a baby, I was an insomniac.

"What about Dad? Did he like taking care of me?"

Mama smiled. "He was the only one who could get you to dreamland. He would throw a blanket over your head and dance you around the living room, swinging you back and forth and singing those crazy rock songs. I was always afraid that he would drop you. Especially when he pushed you on that swing."

The swing in my old backyard was built by my dad, a tire looped with fifty feet of ragged rope. The knots reminded me of cords on Venetian blinds. It scraped my thighs when Dad pushed me to and fro, soaring higher until I imagined flipping over, like a cartoon, and looping around the oak tree.

My mind spun in circles. I glanced around the kitchen. Mama had a pile of junk on the cabinet—a toy car from Taco Bell, a stack of envelopes I assumed were bills, a paintbrush so clean, I knew she had never used it.

For someone obsessed with cleaning, I found it strange that she saved everything. It wasn't much different from my bottle-cap collection. Of course, she had no problem selling my toys at a tag sale.

I looked outside. There was a green glow over the neighbor's backyard, spotlit like a stage. Their pool light was a Cyclops eye hovering above nothing. I saw my own reflection in the sliding-glass door. For a moment, I seemed pale and less than solid, like a ghost.

What He Told Me

In Dr. Calaban's office on Friday, I saw Thayer in the waiting room. I felt funny acknowledging him there, but he saluted me.

"Hey, shortie. What's shaking?"

"I wondered if you'd show up," I blurted.

He laughed, despite the half-dozen patients glaring at us. Or maybe because of it.

"I'm getting my prescription refilled," he said. "I need it to get through today."

"Sounds like you're psychologically hooked on Ritalin," I told him.

"Probably," he agreed. "Hey, there's something I gotta tell you. I'll give you a ring later."

Give me a ring? In my mind, I saw a diamond with a cartoony sparkle. It took me a minute to realize what he meant.

When he finally called after dinner, I saw "Pinsky" on the machine and picked it up before Mama got in the way.

"Thayer?"

"I knew you were psychic," he said.

"Yeah?" I said. I hated talking on the phone.

"Just thought I'd give you a shout and tell you I'm alive. Well, almost alive. I'm in sinus confusion land. I've been taking Benadryl, like, on the hour."

"Well, it's nice to know you weren't abducted by aliens."

"I wish," he said. "Did you know Benadryl was developed as a sedative for mental patients? Mom uses it to drug the dog when our neighbors set off firecrackers on Cinco de Mayo."

I nodded, though nobody could see me nod.

"I tried shots, decongestants, antihistamines, nasal sprays," Thayer said.

In the living room, Mama was watching TV, as usual, calling out answers to a Weather Channel quiz. "What is atmospheric pressure?" She sat in the wicker chair wearing her "South Beach" sweatshirt and jeans. What I really wanted to do was grab her skinny shoulders and tell her to shape up.

"Fin, did you get that?" she yelled.

I picked up the phone and snuck outside. Cordless phones are a miracle.

"Where are you?" Thayer asked.

I closed my eyes. The rainy smell of the leaves drifted to me. "I'm on the porch."

"Let me hear," he said.

"Huh?"

"What does it sound like?"

I lifted the phone and let him listen to the bufo toads croaking in alto.

Thayer coughed a long, rattling cough. He was already in the middle of some randomness.

"Okay. So let's just take tonight, for example, okay? My mom's all attitudey. She caught me smoking pot in the garage and took away my weed, which is actually hers. She's all up in my face while I'm petting the freaking dog. So I go outside to find Bozo's Frisbee. And Mom's all like, 'Thayer, get in here.' God, it's so freaking annoying. She just can't let me be."

I waited for him to finish.

"Are you there?" he said.

"Yes."

"I want to tell you something."

"What?"

I hugged my knees and felt my heart thumping fast.

"I got suspended," Thayer said.

"Again?"

"This time it's bad. Real bad," he said. "I got caught writing up my desk. Then smartass Sharon Lubbitz is like, 'That looks like the graffiti in the girls' bathroom,' as if everyone hadn't already seen it. So basically I'm screwed on many levels."

"How many?"

"Suspension is the least of my problems. My mom's talking military school. And though camouflage is my color, I ain't going."

I was quiet for a minute. Then I opened my mouth.

"I could take the blame. I mean, Sharon's two-faced buddies have caught me doing it."

"Whoa, shortie. You'd front for me? That's mad sweet. But I've got another plan. I'm getting out of here."

I squeezed tighter. He had to be joking. So I joked back.

"Russia is recruiting volunteers to Mars?"

"Uh-uh," he said. "Do you know where I want to go?"

"No clue."

"To New York. That's where my gram lives. Up there, I could finally get something going with my art."

"You mean, like art school?"

"No. I'm going to hook up with a crew and tag all the trains in Brooklyn. School blows. Going to school for art would tell me that, number one, I'm not original, and number two, I'm just a toy. Bottom line, it would be like going to school for breathing."

I thought I was going deaf. "New York is really far away," I said.

"I'll hitchhike. Or take a bus. Hell, I could be there in two days." I heard him suck in a raggedy breath. "I'd give anything to be out of school and on my way to NYC."

Light slipped across the lawn. Mama stood in

242

the door, watching. I sat up and smoothed the wrinkles in my jeans.

"What are you doing alone in the dark?" she said. "Who's that on the phone? You're going to get eaten alive by mosquitoes."

"It's someone from class," I said, "asking about homework."

"What homework?" she said.

"You know. Math and stuff."

Mama didn't look convinced. I could hear the TV's applause before she shut the door.

"What about your mom?" I whispered into the phone.

"Like I said, we got in a fight. Besides, she's never around."

Should I tell someone about his plan? Mama would freak out and call the cops. What if I went with him? I thought about it, thought about joining Thayer at the bus station, leaving school, my teachers, Dr. Calaban. I couldn't do it. I couldn't just get up and leave. Not when I was just starting to get a grip on things.

"Do you think I'm crazy?" he asked.

"Maybe. Maybe not."

"What's that supposed to mean?"

"It means I don't know."

"You think I'm mentally ill."

"I never said that."

"My mom says I can't think in a straight line. She's the one who needs a shrink." He sighed. "I'm sick of school, all those fake people. It's a game. They buy it. I don't."

"Stop," I said.

I was just grasping his words, trying to make sense of it.

"Come with me. You're always saying you don't belong here, down south in the MIA."

I saw the letters floating in my mind. Thayer's nickname for Miami sounded more like "missing in action."

"We can't just leave," I said.

"Man, I thought you were for real."

"I take it back. You are crazy."

"Just for a few days," Thayer said. I could hear a dog barking in the background.

"Which days?"

"Starting now," he said.

I was summoning my numbers when I remembered what Dr. Calaban had said. I couldn't keep everyone safe by counting.

"Please don't go," I said.

I pictured Thayer roaming the streets and sleeping behind Dumpsters.

"I knew you wouldn't understand."

"Thayer, listen to me."

"I'm through listening."

"There's nothing in New York that you don't have here," I said.

Maybe even less.

Escape

I snuck inside the garage. My bike was mounted on the wall. The night was sweltering. If I could get to the bus stop in time, maybe I could talk Thayer out of it.

I rolled my bike out and pushed off. There was a squeak as I tested the brakes, then the soft hiss of the grass. I looked over my shoulder. The windows in my house flickered blue. Mama was probably still watching the Weather Channel or the Food Network, although she hated to cook and never went anywhere. I pumped faster.

At the end of the block, I turned onto US 1. A car behind me honked. I rode past the abandoned house where I took my first dose of Paxil. The FOR SALE sign was gone. Somebody had trimmed the trees.

My legs burned. I rode past the playground, through intersections, and around burger joints. Cars zoomed off of the highway near school. A few older boys were playing basketball, but I didn't stop to watch.

"Hey, bike girl," one of them called.

I kept riding. I saw a Greyhound bus and wondered if Thayer was on it. Traffic was thicker downtown. This is where the skyscrapers began. The gray buildings pressed against one another—perfume outlets, Sunglass Hut, secondhand radios, wholesale jewelry. Homeless people camped near the Miami River Bridge, huddled under cardboard boxes, within spitting distance of the ancient stone Circle.

I focused on the bus station's address, which Thayer had told me. My obsessive-compulsive habits were actually good for something. Four, one, one, one, Northwest Twenty-seventh Street. Twenty was an even number. Seven was odd. I didn't care whether they went together anymore. I had to keep them in place.

A military green truck raced past me. The

driver flicked a cigarette out the window. Sparks crackled on the road.

All this time, I had felt invisible. Now it seemed like everybody was watching.

I eased onto the sidewalk. The green truck was speeding beside me. I could hear the radio squirting out beats. I pedaled harder.

"Want a lift?" said the driver, leaning out.

I shook my head.

"Are you lost?" he asked. He was wearing a denim jacket, oiled gray with dirt. "Need some money?" The guy dangled a balled-up dollar bill.

"No, thanks. I'm going to a friend's house."

The driver laughed. "Sure you are."

I waited for the traffic to thin out, then swerved behind the truck. I pedaled toward a cafetine, a Cuban restaurant where people stood on the sidewalk, sipping high-octane coffee from thimble-sized cups at a window.

There was no place to chain my bike, so I left it leaning against the concrete wall. The cafetine was surrounded. Rows of elderly Hispanic women with plastic bonnets circled like hens at the window.

I stood in line as if buying tickets for a movie. A waitress slapped down a sticky menu in a language that I couldn't read. On the counter was some Nutella, a hazelnut spread. ANNA, read the waitress's name tag.

"What do you want, baby?"

"Nothing," I said. "I mean, do you have a phone I could use?"

She fixed her gaze on me. "There's a pay phone across the street. But it's broken."

"It's an emergency."

"You hiding from someone?"

"Not really," I said.

She dug into her pocket. "Here. Use my cell."

"Thanks," I said. She stood there, watching.

The phone was heavy. I stared at the Tweety Bird sticker peeling above the screen. Normally, I couldn't stand to touch somebody's germy phone, but it didn't matter anymore.

I punched the digits and waited.

The phone clicked and rang a few times. It was Yara on the answering machine, peppering her speech with "please" and "thank you." Mama said

Dad always falls for a woman who says "Bless you" after a sneeze.

Then Yara picked up for real. "Hello. Sorry?"

I heard outer-space noises crackling and Yara saying, "Fin?" Then the cash register jingled.

"Fin? I can hardly hear you. Are you in trouble? Your mom keeps calling. She's frantic."

I nodded, even though she couldn't see me. "I'm okay."

"Talk to me, chica. I promise not to get angry."

I stared past the highway. "I'm at a cafetine. On the corner of Second Street and First Avenue."

"What?" she said. "You ran away?"

"Listen," I said. "There's this boy, my friend, Thayer. He was trying to get on a bus. He's probably gone by now. I tried to find the station but everything is so confusing downtown, all those one-way streets. Then there was this truck driver . . ." I couldn't explain. I had run out of words.

"Stay put. I'll call your mother."

When Yara hung up, I kept holding the phone. I listened to the dial tone, as if it could tell me what to do next.

Frida Kahlo

Your family's coming?" the waitress asked.

"Yeah. *Gracias*," I said, handing back the phone.

Seconds later, she returned with a Styrofoam cup of café con leche and a napkin heaped with sugar-dusted guava pastries. I sipped the coffee, which seemed to glow inside my stomach. I couldn't stop watching the street. The urge to count simmered in my fingers.

I asked Anna for a pen. She reached into her apron and pulled out a blunt felt-tip marker. I flipped over the napkin and started doodling. I drew spiky, punk-style tags and roller-skating robots. I drew Dr. Calaban tangled up with her African violets, Mama sitting in front of a grinning television,

Thayer blowing three perfect smoke rings—zero, zero, zero—with a skinny girl in a bandanna. The ink bled through the paper, ripping into dandrufflike shreds. I didn't feel like tearing the corners to make them even. I kept drawing.

After I had eaten the pastries and filled another napkin with doodles, a Nissan pulled up to the curb. Mama got out with an umbrella, although it was only sprinkling. She yanked me into a hug and held me a long time. When we finally let go, she licked her finger and wiped sugar off my face. Usually this would've sent me over the edge, but I didn't move.

"Well," she said. "You gave me a fright."

"I didn't mean to," I said.

Mama grabbed a fistful of napkins and patted down my hair. She looked at the empty cup of coffee but didn't mention it stunting my growth. She peered over my shoulder and flashed an off-center smile.

"You're quite an artist," she said. "Are you going to be the next Frida Kahlo?"

"Who's that?"

"One of the world's greatest women painters."
She crinkled her nose. "Don't they teach you anything in school?"

A ripple of embarrassment shot through me. "I
haven't taken art in a while."

"When I was your age, I wanted to be a painter.
Even won a scholarship for art school. My father
thought it was a waste of time, so I never went."

I nodded. She had never told me this before. I
guess there was a lot about Mama that I didn't
know.

Mama rubbed her eyes. She took out her pack of
cigarettes, then put them away.

"I'm going to quit," she said.

"Really?" I wasn't sure what to believe.

"You want to tell me what this is all about?" she
asked.

"It's my friend. Thayer. He's gone on a bus."

"Gone? Where?"

"I don't know. He wanted to run away."

"My Lord. What was he thinking?"

Mama waited for an answer I couldn't give. I
leaned back, liking the fact that she was listening.

"Where was he planning to go?"

"New York, I think."

"New York?" She clucked her tongue.

For a moment, we said nothing. Mama looked so exhausted. She hardly ever drove anywhere at night, much less in the rain. It must have been a big deal for her.

"Which bus stop?" she asked. "The one downtown?"

"Yeah. He might be there already." I thought about Thayer riding the Metrorail, snaking above the traffic.

"So why didn't you tell me about this? And why did you try to bike over? Do you realize how dangerous that was?"

I closed my mouth tight.

"Let's go," she said, grabbing her keys.

Manatee

We sped along Biscayne Boulevard. At the end of the road was the bus station. Not really a station, more like a shack, with concrete benches splattered with bird droppings. Mama parked by the curb, even though there was no parking space, and we got out.

The light from the street lamps shone onto the row of buses. I felt my pulse beating in my ears. Graffiti trickled across the bumpers. Had Thayer ever tagged a bus?

Mama followed, huffing as I raced around the lot. By the time we returned to our car, I was out of breath. Nearby, a bunch of kids were shrieking, "Boys come from Jupiter because they're stupider. Girls come from Mars because they're superstars."

Still no Thayer. I could see panic in Mama's face.

"You don't think he did something foolish?" she said.

I searched the parking lot for his dreadlocked hair. It was like he never existed.

"He's not here," I said.

"I think we should call his parents," she said.

"He lives with his mom," I said.

"Well, do you have the phone number?"

I glanced at my hand. "No."

I did, but I didn't want to get Thayer into any more trouble.

"Where else would he go?"

I thought about the canal near our school.

The next thing I knew, Mama and I were in the car again.

"Show me," she said.

We drove past school and slowed when we got to the canal, the one Thayer had shown me. Mama parked near the power plant and we got out.

And there he was, walking toward the canal, smoking, his dreads pulled back like a sphinx. He was whistling something, a cartoon theme song.

I wanted to move, but Mama grabbed my hand so tight, I could hear things popping inside it.

"That's your friend?" she said. The worried tone was back. Her voice made a cramp shoot through my stomach.

"Yeah." I could hear Thayer, his whistling shrill and loud. I nodded and Mama tugged me along.

"Walk quickly," she said. "Don't run."

At first I was frozen. I didn't move. Staring was all I could do. It was dark outside, and all I saw was a thin shadow of Thayer, just the edges. But slowly he took shape, from the dime-sized holes in his floppy jeans, to the half-buttoned plaid shirt and pale hair, to his chin pointed at the water.

I led Mama through the path near the power plant. A rusty sign warned, DANGER! HIGH VOLTAGE! with a scowling lightning bolt. The gate was open, as usual, and we eased through it.

We heard the hiss coming from the plant. Overhead, a plume of smoke bubbled on the horizon. Mama tugged my sleeve.

There was Thayer, waist-deep in the mucky canal.

"Fin?" he called. "How did you get here?"

"I thought you had run away. Like, on a bus."

"Came out here to think," he said. He looked down into the canal. "They drift up here because it's warm."

Thayer was hunched over an oval ring in the water. A manatee.

The beast's spatula-shaped tail made a swirl as she dove. She looked about ten feet long, as old as the dinosaurs, so out of place in that canal near the smoke-belching power plant. Yet this was her home. We were the ones who didn't belong. Still, at that moment, I felt as if I belonged there with her. I wanted to know what she was thinking and if she felt alone, like me.

I made my way toward the canal, sinking up to my knees in mud. I didn't like the look of the brownish tide, or the thought of what was wiggling in it—mosquito larvae, bloodsucking leeches. I could hear Mama calling my name but I didn't listen. I stepped into the water, which was warmer than I imagined. As I shuffled forward, the bottom sloped to a drop. I pushed off and doggy-paddled, my T-shirt ballooning.

I looked over my shoulder to find Mama, but I couldn't trace her in the trees. I got within inches of Thayer when the manatee poked her lumpy snout at me. The aquatic mammal looked like a boulder. I paddled closer, hoping I could coax Thayer out of this mess before we ended up in jail.

I treaded around the canal and again the manatee blocked me. I reached out to touch her, to confirm she wasn't a mirage. She rolled over. Her back was crusted with barnacles and powerboat scars.

As I moved close enough to grab Thayer, he threw his arms around the putty-faced beast. She must've weighed a thousand pounds. I thought she might drag us down, sinking into the tangle of weeds, holding us there until we drowned. But she didn't.

The manatee swerved in my direction. Ducking down, I spied another manatee, a calf, gliding out of the foggy water like a ghost. I rose up, heaving.

I was startled by a splash and turned around. Mama inched into the water. Thayer didn't seem aware of her, not even when she called his name. He was drifting away from all of us.

Thayer started coughing and spitting up mucus. His throat made a whistling sound when he breathed. One, two, three, gasp. We all heard him panting. Up close, his lips and fingernails were a bluish color.

"My lungs," he said. "Burning." His voice was raspy.

Mama twitched, shin-deep in the canal. She wouldn't go any closer.

When Thayer tried to talk, his words were chopped up. "Hurts," he said. "I can't breathe."

He was dodging and paddling, elbows flaring, around the muddy shapes in the water. I tried to reach him, one, two, three times. He went left. I went right. He dodged again and then clenched his arms around me. My heart almost stopped. We were sinking into the murk.

"Kryptonite," he said.

Thayer was still wheezing, all blue.

Grabbing his wrists, I tugged. Then Thayer gasped, "Let go."

We bobbed in the water, soaking wet, our T-shirts floating. The instant I let go, the manatee bumped me. I thought about what Thayer had said. They were trapped in the modern world. But they were surviving, coping in their own way, as Thayer had taught me to do.

A siren grew closer, red lights spinning. Thayer dangled in the water, trapped, and I kept thinking how this should be embarrassing, me in my wet clothes and he paddling there like a wild animal. I saw that he wasn't struggling. We were calm, both of us there, not saying anything, just hanging below the surface.

The silence washed over me like a wave. I didn't have to think anymore. I just drifted, weightless, in the underwater quiet. I could've stayed in that silence forever, coasting in a place where nothing pulled at me, not even gravity.

Then a man grabbed me from behind, invisible, hauling me into light and noise. As I was hoisted up, I sputtered, trying to stand, my legs scissoring under me, searching for something solid.

The ambulance siren cut off.

Lying in the damp grass, I watched the paramedics surround Thayer. I hadn't seen them pull him out. I could barely see his tangled limbs, bent like the number seven. His hands were slightly open, as if cupped to hold water.

A paramedic with Buddha arms tilted Thayer's head back and leaned in. He pinched Thayer's nose, covered his mouth with his own, and blew. One, two breaths. Thayer still wasn't moving. The man pushed down on Thayer's chest, pumping once per second. Two breaths. Fifteen pumps.

The odd-numberness bothered me. My mind latched on to it and conjured a list of things I hated: the smell of chalk, shag carpet, insurance commercials. I counted forward and backward. It wasn't working anymore.

Mama was leaning into the ambulance. We stood against it, watching each other. Across the canal, the water was still.

Mama pulled off her sweatshirt and wrapped it around me like a towel. She was kneeling in the grass, trying to wipe my face. Her hands circled around and around. She held on to me, her entire body shaking.

Someday We Will Go to the Moon

The night before Dad moved out, I watched him drag his homemade telescope on the back porch and look for planets in the sky. Dad had built the telescope out of a cardboard tube. He painted it black to make it look more realistic, but it embarrassed me anyway.

Hunching down, I saw the stubble ringing his head, the neck rolls at the base of his hair. Then his jaw went tight and he unscrewed the lens.

"No good," he said. "Too cloudy. Give it a try later, if you like."

He went inside. Gave up, just like that.

Lights hovered around the block. I looked at the rows of houses lined up by number. I swiveled the telescope, watching, and turned toward the stars swirling in their sockets. Lightning strobed, bright as streamers. If I counted between rumbles and flashes, I could figure out the storm's distance. One hippopotamus, two hippopotamus. Ten seconds was two miles away.

I tried hunting for the moon. People had walked on it, long ago. The moon, a dead place. It looked primitive, the craters reminding me of chalk scribble. I couldn't picture spacemen bouncing across its canyons. Somewhere on its glowing surface, they left a flag, a bunch of souped-up space buggies, and their footprints. When Dad was little, he saw it on TV. I used to laugh when I thumbed through his outdated astronomy books. *Someday,* read the last page, *we will go to the moon.*

In lunar time, everybody would age more slowly. When we stared at the night sky, and happened to spot the moon, its bruised edges, the shadowy oceans, I knew this much: The moon was always there, even when I couldn't see it.

A second ambulance whisked Mama and me away. We rode with the paramedics. Mama told them not to take us to the hospital where a doctor had left a sponge in a patient's leg. She started jabbering about Dad leaving us.

"Do you want me to call him?" I asked.

"No," she said.

I sat in the waiting room, shivering for three hours. One hundred and eighty minutes. I didn't talk to anyone. I thought about Thayer, the teapot whistling in his chest, the incredible weight of him in the canal.

I looked at the photographs in *Sky and Telescope* magazine—Martian volcanoes, sombrero-shaped asteroids, cartwheeling galaxies, and the Hubble's broken gyroscopes. In some way, I tried to bind them together, even the telescope with its busted discs. They were like my invisible army of numbers. Although I couldn't see them, they were always there, like the daytime moon or the tennis ball hidden in our classroom. My OCD had left me feeling out of control. Now I was taking control of it.

I got hold of Dad and told him what was going on. He tried to take my mind off of it by telling me about Yara's family.

"They're really looking forward to meeting you, grasshopper. You're going to love the Ortiz familia. On Sundays the old guys, all the grandfathers, get together and smoke cigars and play dominoes. It gets really intense, you know? And you should see the amount of food they make. It's all about fresh fish. They'll take you out on the boat . . . ," he said, his voice trailing off. He didn't finish his sentence. I suppose he forgot that water wasn't exactly my friend.

I couldn't stand to hurt his feelings. So I asked, "What kind of food do they make? Yara's family, I mean?"

"Oh, it's to die for," he said, perking up again. "You've got paella, which is a rice casserole with all kinds of yummy seafood in it. You can eat it right out of the pan with a spoon."

"Sounds good," I said.

After we hung up, I made a pact to try a little harder with Yara. If she was going to be around, I might as well get to know her better.

I sat in a hard, plastic chair until someone tapped my arm. It was Thayer's mom, Mrs. Pinsky, a tall woman, thin as a chopstick. Her pale hair was tugged back with a sequined barrette.

"You're Thayer's friend." Her face was puffy from crying.

She said he was in intensive care, hooked up to machines to help him breathe. But he was going to be fine.

"Machines?" I said. My eyelashes were damp.

Mrs. Pinsky tugged her barrette. "He's had severe asthma his whole life," she said. "I've yanked out the carpets in my house. In Thayer's case, that's not the problem. It's the weather. Especially if there's haze."

I rubbed my eyes.

"He was looking for manatees," I said.

Mrs. Pinsky wasn't listening. "If I don't have an inhaler handy, a cup of black coffee does the trick."

"Thayer hates coffee," I said.

I could hear her breathing. On the TV strapped to the wall, a police siren wailed.

"He asked me to find you," she said.

"That's cool," I said.

I stared at the floor. The linoleum, along with

every gleaming surface, was white.

Mrs. Pinsky coughed and said, "I'll tell Thayer hello for you."

She touched me again, on the arm. Usually, my numbers would've been glowing, getting ready to guide my hand, touch the opposite side and balance things out. But this time, I kept still. All of me did.

Fin

Over the weekend, Mama took care of me. She said the afterlife would come sooner than later if I didn't get something to eat, so we nuked a plate of eggs in the microwave. While the flabby yolks popped and sizzled, Mrs. Pinsky called to say Thayer was feeling better and wouldn't I like to visit him in the hospital? I imagined his room. White tiles. Sick people on stretchers.

I looked at my plate and pushed it away. We still had three eggs left in the carton. Mama said we could bake a cake with them.

"From scratch?" I asked.

"Why not?" Mama was already bustling in the cupboard.

"I didn't think you knew how," I said.

"Your grandmother taught me when I was your age. Now it's my turn to teach you," she said, inspecting a dusty bottle of vanilla extract. "Are you ready for this?"

I wasn't sure.

Mama showed me how to crack an egg with one hand. "Tap on a flat surface instead of an edge," she said, thumping it on my head.

We added leftover Halloween candy, Milky Ways and M&Ms, to the mix. Mama said cooking was like painting with flavors instead of colors. She didn't care when I cranked up the radio, not even when I turned the dial from smooth jazz to a screamy college radio station.

She let me lick the bowl, just like when I was little. Mama traced her finger along the rim and smeared chocolate on my face. I chased her around the kitchen, giggling as she wiggled away from me. We were so busy jumping around, we forgot about the cake.

Mama opened her eyes wide. I figured she was upset about the mess. Then she glanced at me and said, "Uh-oh."

When we cracked open the oven, I saw a rectangular lump in the bottom of the pan. The cake came out like a flat brick, but we frosted it anyway.

"Do we have to eat it?" I asked.

"Let's just look at it for a while," she said, smiling.

In the hospital's waiting room, a TV played *The Price Is Right*, all those spangled numbers blurring down the Big Wheel.

Mama steered me into the hallway, which stank of Pine-Sol. The wallpaper was crawling with palm trees and pink flamingos, someone's half-baked idea of a tropical landscape.

"Let's go back," I said, earning a freezing look from Mama.

The elevator arrived with an electric ding. The walls withdrew. A nurse stepped out. She wore a glittery Santa pin on her collar.

Mama and I got in. I pushed the UP arrow. The seven was just a seven, no magic power. I was still noticing numbers, but they did nothing for me. And though I wanted to wash my hands really bad, I knew it could wait. The control-freak section of my brain was like the tennis ball hidden in our classroom, there but not there, the way a song got stuck in my head. I was learning to ignore the song without mood-altering drugs. No more Paxil. But I didn't want to stop talking to Dr. Calaban, not when I had so much more to say.

The elevator squeaked and clattered. Through the door, a sliver of light flickered like a malfunctioning slide show. I imagined that by pressing a button, I had caused the entire hospital to sink into the ground while we stayed still. We landed on the top floor with a thunk.

Thayer's room was around the corner. He didn't have a tube shoved down his throat or a machine breathing for him. He was humming along with the television.

Mama nudged me. "Go on," she said. "I'll wait."

He turned. His dreads were pulled back tight.

I forced a smile.

Thayer kept quiet.

"How's it going?" I asked.

He put his hand over mine, warming me up. Only then did I notice the scars on his wrists, pale crescents where doctors had plunged needles.

"What are you doing here?" he said, coughing.

All the blood in my body rushed to my face.

But then he said, "I'm glad you came."

A wave swelled inside my throat. I tried to swallow it.

"I brought your science homework. It's on gravity."

"What goes up must come down," Thayer said. "Yo, what else you need to know?" He stared at me, blinking, waiting.

"That's not all." I reached into my pocket and pulled out the stone.

He grinned. "You go first."

"I didn't realize," I said. "I didn't realize your asthma was so bad."

"It's cool," he said.

"No, it's not," I said.

A bubble of silence quivered around us.

"You're a good swimmer," he said.

"Not good enough." I thought for a moment. "I'm never going there again, ever. Not even to see the manatees."

Thayer laughed a little. So did I. If the nurse knew we were laughing about almost running away and drowning in a canal, she would think we were crazy. It didn't matter what other people thought. I was learning not to worry about it.

When we finally stopped to catch our breath, I noticed this one lone freckle, splashed on his collarbone. I put my hand there and he kissed my fingers. Then he kissed up my arm, like they do in cartoons. Then he kissed me, really softly, on the lips.

"I like you," he whispered. He wasn't holding the stone, but I knew he was telling the truth.

I got so nervous, I shoved my hand in my pocket. Folded inside was the rain-stained napkin I had been doodling on at the cafetine. And then it was all clear to me. Clear like the night sky in Dad's telescope, cold and bright. It was okay to feel nervous. Something was starting to happen, something beyond my control, and I liked it.

"Let's see," said Thayer.

Thayer and I took turns sketching until the paper shimmered with ink.

"I'm keeping this for eternity," he said.

"An eternity is a long time." I smirked.

"Remember what I told you? There's no such thing as time," he said.

I looked out the window. The parking lot glistened.

Thayer said that his mom had called a truce. She wasn't shipping him off to military school, but he would start fresh at a private Catholic academy, Columbus, after winter vacation. I couldn't picture Thayer in pleated khakis with a tie looped around his neck.

"I'm giving up weed," he said. "I had to promise."

I couldn't picture that, either.

"Know what else I promise?" he said, leaning closer. "I'm going to visit you every day at lunch."

"You're going to skate ten miles so we can eat in the music room," I said. "Right. I believe that."

"Who said anything about skating?" He winked.

"So you're going to flap your arms and fly?"

"If that's what it takes," he said. And this I could picture.

* * *

I didn't speak to Mama until we left the hospital.

"Want to take a walk?" I asked.

She smiled. "When you were a kid, we used to go for walks every afternoon."

"Dad took me," I said.

"I remember," she said. "You got stung by a bee once."

"It was a hornet."

"No. A bee. You collected soda tabs for me. We made a necklace out of them. I still have it."

I looked up. "Really? I didn't know that."

I took Mama to the empty house. Maybe it was my last chance to see it before the new people moved in there. The hurricane shutters had finally come off. Everywhere we looked were concrete blocks. Some were painted Day-Glo colors, the kind you'd probably see on an island like Haiti. On the front lawn was something new: a tire swing.

"Looks like a family is almost ready to move in," Mama said.

At first, she hadn't understood why I wanted to take her here. "It's just a quiet place to talk," I had explained.

"Your quiet place," she said.

"It was."

Land crabs scuttled into mud holes, making dry clacking noises. I decided to trudge into the foliage around the side of the house, despite Mama shouting, "That's full of holly berries. You'll break out in a rash. Don't step on the leaves. If you do, wipe your feet on the grass."

Usually, I'd be simmering, getting ready to shout back. Instead, I just let her be.

We headed back toward the empty house, our hair threaded with leaves. Cicadas droned overhead, a noise not unlike a power saw. They lived seventeen years underground and died after sprouting wings.

I squinted at the lava-colored sky. Miami had the coolest sunsets. That much I had to admit.

"There's a star. Two of them peeking out," I said, wondering if the sunset really did contain lithium. Maybe Dr. Calaban knew the answer.

"I see," Mama told me.

I watched her wade through a sea of saw grass. A hot breeze rippled the brush, making a noise like my violin. We stood there, staring at the sky. What we saw I wasn't sure. Counting stars was like wishing on nothing. By now, they may have burned out, leaving their light behind like a signature in Magic Marker.

I could never count them all.

I don't wanna be a number
I just wanna stay free

—"Numbers," the Adicts

Mad props

My agent, Kate Lee, for understanding the kind of story I wanted to tell and keeping it real.

My editors, Julie Lansky and Katherine Tegen, whose suggestions were always on the mark. This book would not exist without you.

I'm grateful to the Bread Loaf Writers' Conference, the Rutgers One on One Council, and SCBWI for showing me the way.

Joy Bagley, Ben Barnes, Patricia Dolan, John Maass, Bill Rothman, Evelyn Mayerson, May-Lin Svantesen, and Joyce Sweeney, who put up with the pages in their mailboxes and encouraged me from the start. Also thanks to my rock star students, Dr. Aaron Gleason for the psychological insight, Adrian Michna and Secret Frequency Crew for the soundtrack, and Harlan Erskine, for always listening.

And to my wonderful, crazy family, especially Jonathan Chappell ("knowledge is a tree"); my father, Raymond, who read to me; and my mother, Joann, who believed in invisible friends.